"I'd Like To See The Will." She Did Her Best To Keep The Tension Out Of Her Voice, To Keep It Level And Professional. To Her Annoyance, Her Pulse Kicked Up.

He drew a leather document holder from under his arm. A surreptitious glance revealed lines of tiredness etched deep into his face, though they failed to mute the impact of his hard, handsome features.

Unable to restrain herself, Victoria snatched up the will, scanning the headings as she flicked through the pages. Searching for proof a darling baby's life had changed forever.

"Co-guardian." His voice was gravelly, all male, full of edges with no smooth sweetness. "And we share custody, too."

A gust of chilly wind cut through the fabric of her dress. She shivered. Crossing her arms, she let the will fall as she rubbed her hands absently up and down her body.

Joint custody and co-guardianship. How on earth was that going to work? Damn, what had her friend been thinking?

Dear Reader,

I'll never forget the day that my first child was born. The doctor placed this wailing little person on my chest and I greeted him. The screams stopped instantly. He grew still. The nurse and my husband began to laugh, and the doctor said, "He knows his mom's voice." As I carried on talking, my baby tried to lift his head to look at me. I knew then that the doctor was right. All those months that he'd been part of me, he'd learned the sound of my voice. And right there a bond was forged.

It was an amazingly profound moment for me.

So it probably won't surprise you that I've always enjoyed romances that contain babies. There is a tenderness in these stories—and often the stakes are so much higher. It's not only the hero and heroine's relationship that's at risk, but the future of that vulnerable baby, too.

I'm a huge fan of Silhouette Desire's BILLIONAIRES AND BABIES stories…I have read all the titles published so far…and I'm thrilled that Connor and Victoria's story is part of this fabulous collection. Check out my Web site, www.tessaradley.com, for a chance to win Maureen Child's *Baby Bonanza* and Emily McKay's *Baby Benefits* in one volume…if you haven't already added these stories to your keeper shelf!

Happy reading!

Tessa Radley

TESSA RADLEY

BILLION-DOLLAR BABY BARGAIN

Published by Silhouette Books
America's Publisher of Contemporary Romance

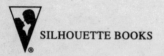

SILHOUETTE BOOKS

ISBN-13: 978-0-373-76961-2

BILLION-DOLLAR BABY BARGAIN

Visit Silhouette Books at www.eHarlequin.com

Printed in U.S.A.

Please recycle
THIS PRODUCT IS RECYCLABLE

Recycling programs
for this product may
not exist in your area.

TESSA RADLEY

loves traveling, reading and watching the world around her. As a teen Tessa wanted to be an intrepid foreign correspondent. But after completing a bachelor of arts degree and marrying her sweetheart, she became fascinated by law and ended up studying further and practicing as an attorney in a city practice.

A six-month break traveling through Australia with her family reawoke the yen to write. And life as a writer suits her perfectly; traveling and reading count as research, and as for analyzing the world...well, she can think "what if?" all day long. When she's not reading, traveling or thinking about writing, she's spending time with her husband, her two sons, or her zany and wonderful friends. You can contact Tessa through her Web site, www.tessaradley.com.

For my boys

Prologue

Who would have thought that a baby—cute and gurgly when his mother held him—could be such a demanding little devil? Victoria Sutton sank down onto the couch in the living room of her Auckland town house and gazed at the sleeping baby in the traveling cot with weary disbelief.

Dylan looked utterly angelic as stubby eyelashes rested in dusky crescents against chubby baby cheeks and his mouth moved gently up and down.

Oh, for a shot of caffeine.

Strong, hot Starbucks coffee. Hard to believe the whole weekend had passed without finding time to pick one up. Mandy, her secretary, would laugh herself silly tomorrow when Victoria recounted the events of the past two days.

Had it only been two days?

Propping her elbows on her knees, Victoria rested her chin in her palms, and groaned. Two days, but also two pretty much sleepless nights during which Dylan had turned her normally organized life upside down. Heavens, it seemed like she hadn't drawn a breath since her best friend Suzy had gabbled her last bits of advice on Friday evening as Michael had tugged his wife out the front door, eager to get away for a brief romantic break to celebrate their second wedding anniversary.

Never again would she imagine that babies slept all the time!

Lifting her head from her cupped palms, Victoria scanned the normally immaculate living room and took in the chaotic disarray of toys, diapers and other baby paraphernalia. Another groan escaped. She knew her bedroom looked worse. She needed to get the mess packed up before Dylan's parents arrived to collect him.

Victoria glanced ruefully at the apple puree smears on the winter-white fabric of the couch. And that stain on the carpet hadn't been there before Friday, either. What had possessed her to feed Dylan in the all-white living room this morning? Had she learned nothing over the past two days?

Tomorrow first thing she'd organize to get the marks cleaned.

Tomorrow. Oh, heavens. Victoria's hands shot to her mouth in dismay.

The weekly Monday-morning partners' meeting…

Good grief, she hadn't done any preparation. She thought wildly of how she'd delusionally planned to work while Dylan napped over the weekend.

A glance at the wall clock showed her it was still early. Michael and Suzy would be here within the next two hours to pick up Dylan. The whole evening lay ahead.

If she worked quickly to tidy the apartment, she might even get some work in before the Masons arrived. Grabbing a nappy bag, Victoria started to toss in toys, wet-wipes and unused diapers.

But nothing could take away from the fun she'd had with

her godson. They'd played peekaboo and she'd tickled Dylan's tummy. They'd been to the beach, where she'd dipped Dylan's toes in the shallows while he squealed in ecstasy. They'd even shared an ice-cream cone—granted, most of it had ended up over Dylan's face, plus a few smears down Victoria's favorite Kate Sylvester T-shirt.

So she'd willingly offer to do it again. Her godson was adorable. A memory of his loud, growling screams in the middle of the night made her amend that statement. *Mostly* he was adorable.

The throaty roar of a powerful motor pulling up outside her town house unit made her pause in the act of retrieving a miniature sock from under the coffee table.

She checked the slim gold watch on her wrist. Too early for Michael and Suzy.

The doorbell rang in a long, insistent buzz. Victoria leaped to her feet, a quick glance showing that Dylan hadn't stirred. The bell buzzed again. She shot across the room and, without pausing to look through the peephole, yanked the door open before whoever it was could lean on the doorbell again.

"Connor!"

Connor North, Michael's best man, stood on her doorstep.

To Victoria's annoyance her pulse kicked up, but with practiced ease she avoided Connor's gaze. He wore a white T-shirt that stretched across a broad chest, and a pair of jeans that molded the lean hips.

"I probably should have called."

His voice was gravelly, all male, full of edges with no smooth sweetness. Victoria knew she should reply, should agree that it would have been better for him to have called first—and then hope like blazes that he would go.

Instead, unable to answer him or steel herself to meet his unsettling pale gray eyes, Victoria fixed her gaze on the hard line of his mouth. *Mistake.* It had been two years since he had kissed her at Michael and Suzy's wedding. By rights she should've forgotten all about the texture of his lips against hers, the desire that had spun dizzily within her.

She hadn't.

Victoria swallowed.

The memory of the taste of him, the hardness of his body against hers, was so immediate it could've happened yesterday. Despite her every effort to pretend it had never happened at all.

"Connor…" she croaked, wishing he was a million miles away.

Why had he come? They didn't have the kind of relationship that allowed for casual drop-ins. To be honest they didn't have any kind of relationship at all.

Since the wedding the two of them had developed an unspoken pact of practicing avoidance: when one arrived at the Masons' home, the other departed within minutes. The passage of time had not dulled the hostility that crackled between them. A dislike that they both colluded to conceal from Michael and Suzy—and Dylan.

She tried again. "Connor, what are you doing here?"

Carefully, with immense composure, she raised her gaze from that hard, tight mouth and met his gaze. To her astonishment he didn't look anything like his usual arrogant, assured self. He looked…

She took in his pallor, the dull flatness in his gray eyes. He looked shattered. "Hey, are you okay?"

"Victoria—" He broke off and shoved his hands in his pockets.

At least he seemed to have no difficulty remembering her name these days, Victoria thought wryly. But it wasn't like Connor to be at a loss for words. Usually the sarcastic quips rolled off his tongue. She frowned. "What is it?"

"Can I come in?"

Victoria hesitated. She didn't particularly want him in her home. But he was…he wasn't himself. "Sure."

Leading him into the living room, she felt a flare of embarrassment at what he must see. Toys. Baby blankets. Dirty plates. She would've preferred Connor to see her home as it normally looked. Elegant. Immaculate. "Excuse the mess."

He didn't even glance sideways. "Victoria…" That soulless gaze was focused on her face with an intensity that was awfully disconcerting.

The need to fill the awkward silence made her blurt out, "Can I fix you a cup of coffee? Not that it's anything like Starbucks, but I was about to make myself—" she stopped before she could reveal that one small human had reduced her to a caffeine-craving wreck "—a hot drink."

"No."

"Tea?"

He shook his head.

She moved toward the kitchen, which opened off the living room, flipped the kettle's switch and opened the fridge.

"I don't have beer. Would you like a cola?" she offered with reluctance as his footfalls sounded on the tiles behind her. She wished he'd waited for her in the living room. There wasn't enough space in the kitchen for the two of them.

"Please." He rubbed a hand over the back of his neck and shut his eyes. An instant later they flicked open and she glimpsed…pain?

Victoria swung away and yanked the fridge door open. She stared blindly at the contents before reaching for two cans of cola. Shutting the door, she said more curtly than she'd intended, "So what do you want, Connor?"

His mouth twisted. "Certainly not sympathy."

She flicked him a rapid once-over as she set the cans down on the counter. He made no move toward the drinks. A ring of white that she hadn't noticed before surrounded his lips.

What was wrong with him? "Why on earth would I offer you sympathy?"

It couldn't possibly be about his former girlfriend. That had been over two years ago and no one ever spoke about Dana or Paul Harper, Connor's former business partner who had pinched his live-in lover while Connor had been out of the country on a business trip.

What Victoria had gleaned of the affair had come from a soft-focus women's magazine feature on Dana and Paul not long after Suzy's wedding. Connor's ex had been nominated for a business award, and was quoted gushing about how happy she was, how she'd "come into herself." There'd been an accompanying spread of photos showing the couple at home in a modern Italianate mansion, all glass and marble.

Yet according to stories in business publications, Harper-North Architecture hadn't thrived well under Paul's leadership after Connor had walked out. In fact, Suzy had once told Victoria that Paul Harper still owed Connor money. Victoria had surmised that the only thing keeping Connor from placing Harper-North—and Paul Harper—into receivership must be his intent to squeeze every cent he could out of Paul Harper.

By contrast, there'd been quite a splash in the media about The Phoenix Corporation, the waterfront development company that Connor had floated. Reading between the lines, Victoria had gathered that he'd turned what for a lesser man might have spelled disaster into a multimillion-dollar success story.

Yet a sense that something was not quite right closed in on her, as he rubbed his hands over his face in a manner she could only describe as helpless.

"I shouldn't have made that crack about sympathy," he said. "Oh, hell, let me start over." He dropped his hands to his sides and the eyes that met hers were as expressionless as ever. "I'm sorry, Victoria, I've got bad news."

"Bad news?" Bewilderment set in. "What bad news?"

"Michael—"

"*No*," she interrupted, as if that might stop her absorbing the reality of the despair that clung to him. "Not Michael!"

Her index finger tapped her watch face with insistent, staccato force. "He'll be here soon. I know it."

Connor was shaking his head and his face was gray, his eyes drained of all vitality. "He won't. He's never coming back."

He had to be.

A sickening fear hollowed out her stomach. She found herself standing right in front of him—closer than she'd ever been, except for that brief disastrous time when they'd danced together at Michael and Suzy's wedding. And when he'd kissed her. "You're wrong."

Because if Michael wasn't coming back that meant...

Seized by desperation, she choked out, "Suzy. Where's Suzy?"

"Victoria..."

This time he didn't have to say anything more. It was all in the way he looked at her with deep sorrow and regret.

"No!" she howled, her throat thickening with grief.

He moved swiftly forward. "Suzy's gone, too."

Victoria fell forward against the broad chest, uncaring of how unyielding Connor's solid frame had become. After a moment of blubbering her arms crept up about his neck.

He grew more rigid still for just a moment until his arms came around her and squeezed. Then he shook off her clinging arms and stepped back, his eyes remote.

"There are arrangements to make. I need to get on to them but I thought you should know..." His voice trailed away.

"That Michael and Suzy are—" she couldn't bring herself to say it "—are not coming home."

A muscle moved high in his cheek. "That's right."

"No, it isn't right. It's wrong!"

The eyes that met hers were full of torment. "Victoria—"

She shook her head. "They're supposed to knock on the door…Suzy will be laughing, she'll call out, 'I'm baaack.'"

He hunched his shoulders.

The lump in her throat finally got too big and her voice broke. Tears welled up from deep within her aching heart. "It's not fair. They should be here."

Backing out of the kitchen, Connor spread his hands, then dropped them to his sides. "Look, there's a lot to be done."

"And you don't have time for good, old-fashioned grief," Victoria said bitterly, as she followed him.

"You're overreacting." He looked hunted. "I'll talk to you later."

"I'm coming with you."

"No, you're not. I work faster alone. And you need to take care of Dylan."

Dylan!

She gaped at Connor in horror. Oh, dear Lord, how could she have forgotten about Dylan?

Dylan had lost his parents.

Connor couldn't leave now. "Connor!"

But Connor was already halfway across the living room. He threw an unreadable glance over his shoulder but didn't slow down. "When I come back we'll talk about Dylan."

One

The taxi pulled up outside the quaint white church where Suzy and Michael would be getting married tomorrow. Victoria paid the driver and leapt out, tugging her rollaway suitcase behind her.

"Hey, Victoria, over here." Suzy stood in the churchyard, waving madly from behind a white-painted wooden gate, her curly blond hair bubbling about her face. "I'm so glad you made it."

"Me, too."

Opening the gate, Victoria abandoned her suitcase and stretched her arms out wide to give Suzy a fierce hug.

"When my plane was delayed I thought I was going to miss the wedding rehearsal." She'd been away doing an audit for one of her largest clients. The text message from Suzy that she was getting married in five days' time had shaken

Victoria—although in hindsight it shouldn't have. Over the past month, everything Suzy said had been prefaced by "Michael says." But Victoria hadn't expected the romance to escalate so quickly. "You certainly decided to get married in a hurry, didn't you?"

Stepping away, Suzy grabbed Victoria's hand. "Come see what the church committee is doing with the flowers."

"You're changing the subject," Victoria said with fond frustration.

Suzy cast her a grin. "Tory, it's too late to try and talk me out of marrying Michael tomorrow."

Victoria smiled at the woman she'd pulled from more scrapes than she cared to remember. "Well, I hope Michael knows what he's letting himself in for. Is he here yet?"

"He and Connor—his best man—" Suzy tacked on at Victoria's questioning glance, "are on their way. We're taking you both out to dinner tonight to celebrate. I booked a table at Bentley's." She did a little jig. "I can't believe it's the last night we'll spend apart. Michael can't wait for tomorrow, either. Come on."

"Wait, let me grab my bag." With a laugh, Victoria reached for the bag and let Suzy lead her through a courtyard overflowing with ivy and rambling roses, rolling her bag behind her.

The late afternoon sun filtered through the branches of a lofty Norfolk pine, casting shadows across the sundial in the centre of the courtyard.

Victoria came to a halt. Suzy slowed. "What now?"

"Suz, don't you think it might've been better to wait? You've only—"

"Known Michael for a month," interrupted Suzy, finishing the sentence with the familiar ease that came from twenty-four years of friendship, "but I knew after an hour that he was The One."

"But Suz—"

Suzy stamped her foot, managing to look sweet and determined at the same time. "No, don't say anything more. Just be happy for us. Please."

Now, how on earth was she supposed to withstand Suzy's puppy-dog eyes? Truth was she'd never been able to say no to Suzy, despite the fact that Victoria was supposed to be the sensible one.

The sound of footsteps prevented Victoria from responding. She glanced around and her eyes widened.

It wasn't Michael—much as she liked him—who snagged her attention, but rather the dark-haired man who strode into the churchyard beside him. Tall and powerfully built with features that could've been carved from granite—angled cheekbones, a blade of a nose and a hard mouth—he made the hair on the back of her neck stand up.

Victoria recognized the animal. She'd met them, done audits for the super-successful companies.

A tycoon.

Rich. Assured. Ruthless.

And this was Michael's best man? Edging slowly forward, she glanced from one man to the other.

Michael's fair good looks dimmed against the other man's dark strength. They were as different as day from night. Where had Michael found him?

She must have said something because his gaze met hers. That was when her stomach flipped over. In contrast to his swarthy skin his pale-gray eyes held the unnerving translucence of crystal. But they contained utterly no emotion.

Ruthless.

"Connor North."

He spoke in a crisp baritone, and Victoria instantly recognized the name. From its outset Harper-North Architecture had garnered buzz and awards for innovative restoration of

Victorian homesteads and plans for cutting-edge new commercial buildings.

With reluctance Victoria took the hand he held out. A hard hand ridged with calluses clasped hers—hardly the hand of an office-bound paper pusher.

Yet from everything she'd heard, Connor North was very much a corporate animal. Financially astute, frighteningly efficient and with an uncanny talent for picking projects that would become landmarks. There was certainly no need for him to busy himself with the manual labor that the ridges on his palms suggested he did. The man was worth a fortune—and accumulating more. Last she'd heard Harper-North was considering launching a commercial-property venture to develop many of Auckland's old dockside warehouses into exclusive waterfront retail complexes. It would be a feather in her cap to land him as a client—and no doubt he'd be able to introduce her to some of the blue-chip companies he was associated with. One or two more accounts like that and she'd be propelled into the upper echelons of Archer, Cameron & Edge.

He glanced down pointedly at their joined hands. A flare of embarrassment seared her as Victoria realized she still clutched his hand. Daydreaming. She dropped it as if she'd been scorched by a flaming torch.

Even Suzy was staring at her. "Do you two know each other?"

Victoria shook her head, not trusting her voice.

"No." Connor North clearly didn't suffer from the same affliction.

"Connor, meet Suzy's oldest friend, Victoria Sutton." Michael gave her an easy smile. "Despite his reputation, Connor won't bite."

Victoria wasn't so sure. Connor North looked capable of doing a lot worse than biting.

"Victoria is a partner at ACE," Michael informed Connor.

Victoria knew she should be grateful for the punt, because

she should be doing everything she could to land his very lucrative account.

Instead, when Connor gave her the opportunity of a lifetime by asking, "The accounting firm?" she could only manage a nod, not trusting her voice. Her stomach, thankfully, seemed to have recovered from the tumbling sensation that had shaken her when she had first looked into his eyes.

Bridget Edge, managing partner of Archer, Cameron & Edge Accounting, would be horrified to see her now. Faced with the opportunity of a lifetime, Victoria couldn't think of anything vaguely professional to say. All she could think of was getting as far away from the man as she could. He made her feel…the best word she could come up with was…*unsettled*.

Still prickling with a mix of apprehension and a weird kind of tingling sensation, Victoria allowed Suzy to shepherd her up the stone stairs into the church while Michael disappeared to put her suitcase in his car.

Inside the church a group of elderly ladies busily arranging white lilies and pristine long-stemmed roses in tall flower stands greeted Suzy with cries of delight. When Michael returned there were chirps about how fortunate he was to be marrying Suzy, and Victoria saw Connor North's mouth turn down at the corners.

He didn't want Michael to marry Suzy!

The realization rocked Victoria. How could anyone disapprove of dear, sweet Suzy?

For the next fifteen minutes Michael smiled indulgently while Suzy cheerfully ordered everyone around and Connor grew increasingly remote.

His phone rang six times while Suzy talked nonstop. Each time, Connor pulled his cell phone out of his pocket, glanced at it, then let it continue to ring.

Victoria could feel herself growing tenser as Connor's disapproving silence continued, and she was ready to scream by the time Suzy called a halt, finally satisfied that the groom, the groomsman and the maid of honor knew what was expected of them.

"I want tomorrow to be perfect." Suzy dimpled a smile at Victoria and moved on to include Connor, too. "Michael and I just want to thank the church ladies for the wonderful job they've done with the flowers, then we'll meet you outside."

"We've been dismissed." Connor gave a grimace that Victoria supposed passed for a smile and stood aside for her to walk ahead of him up the aisle.

Conscious of him stalking behind her, Victoria increased her pace.

As they neared the vestibule his phone rang again. He checked it and this time said, "Excuse me, Verity, I have to take this call."

Victoria pursed her lips. "Victoria."

Connor North stared at her blankly with all the interest of someone examining a moth on the wall. It did nothing to endear him to her. She'd been away on an audit all week. She was hot, tired and he had her in such a tizz, while he barely knew she existed.

"Victoria," she repeated tersely. "My name is Victoria."

His gaze raked her and Victoria became aware that her white blouse was creased from the flight, that her long, straight black skirt clung to her hips and must make her look like a scrawny scarecrow. She ran her fingers past her ears, through her hair, and was relieved to find that the shoulder-length bob was as sleek as ever.

"Sure." Connor shrugged dismissively, and turned away to answer his cell phone.

Victoria followed slowly as he strode out of the church, knowing she ought to care that he'd seen her annoyance. After all, he would be an A-list client. But did she want to deal with him?

No, she decided.

In fact, she could think of nothing worse.

Verity, indeed! Clearly all women were interchangeable in his mind. Like gray cats in the night....

Startled, she pulled her thoughts up short. Where had that come from? There was no chance she would ever be one of Connor North's gray cats. Although his women would be far from gray. No doubt he was the kind of man who went for decorative, desirable D-cups.

A rueful downward glance reminded her that she would be no contender.

Skinny. Beanstalk. Swot. Four-eyes. She had to remind herself that the ugly labels were no longer true, and that only Suzy knew that pathetic creature had ever existed. It was ancient history. In the past. Now she held a partnership in a well-respected accounting firm. No one could take that away from her. She'd fought for it, not allowing cruel, childish taunts or her neglectful parents to roadblock her journey to success...and independence.

Forcing herself not to dwell on the old, self-destructive memories, Victoria fixed a bright smile to her face as she stepped through the carved church doors to the vestibule where Connor paced, his cell phone glued to his ear. She let the scent of lavender hedges in the courtyard outside swirl around her, and slowly serenity returned.

"Michael and Suzy have booked a table to take us to dinner," she told Connor when his call ended, in case he planned to bolt off on a hot date, forgetting all about the bridal couple.

His mouth flattened. "I'm quite sure Michael and Suzy would prefer to spend a quiet evening together before the rush of tomorrow's wedding."

Why hadn't she thought of that?

As they started down the stone steps that led to the courtyard, Victoria noticed with surprise that Connor dwarfed her. It wasn't often that a man made her feel downright dainty.

In the courtyard Suzy and Michael caught up to them. After tomorrow Victoria knew their friendship would never be the same again. A sense of loss filled her, yet she'd never seen Suzy look happier.

She remembered Connor's clever suggestion. "Wouldn't the two of you prefer to have dinner alone tonight?"

Suzy dumped a basket of hymn books into Victoria's arms. "Here, you'll need to give these to the ushers to hand out tomorrow at the door. And of course we want to take the two of you out—we'll have the rest of our lives to spend alone together." Suzy gave Michael a bittersweet smile and Victoria wondered if he, too, had seen the shadows in Suzy's eyes as she spoke…or knew the reason for them.

The way he put an arm across Suzy's shoulders and pulled her close suggested he did. "Victoria, you're Suzy's oldest friend, and Connor's the closest thing I've got to a brother. It will be great for the four of us to have dinner together."

Michael was so nice, Victoria decided. Maybe Suzy hadn't made a mistake. About to give Michael a grateful smile for setting to rest the doubts that Connor had raised, Victoria paused as she intercepted the glacial look Connor shot Michael.

What was that about?

Yet Michael, bless him, smiled in the face of Connor's icy disapproval. He clapped a hand on his best man's shoulder and leant forward to murmur something that caused Connor's pale eyes to flare with suppressed emotion as he shot Victoria a look of intense dislike.

What had she done to deserve *that?* The unexpected unease he'd already roused in her coalesced into a hard ball of antipathy.

As Michael went to fetch his car, Suzy added, "After dinner I'm going home—alone." She winked suggestively at

Victoria. "I told Michael it's unlucky for him to see the bride before the wedding and I'm determined not to do anything that might tip the scales against us."

"You shouldn't be getting married if you need superstitious hocus-pocus to make it last," Connor said from behind them, causing both women to start.

As surprise—followed swiftly by hurt—flashed in Suzy's eyes, Victoria swung around and saw no levity in the man's strange eyes.

Outraged that he'd attacked sweet, effervescent Suzy the moment Michael had vanished, she forgot her own reservations about the hasty marriage. Coldly she pointed out, "But Suzy and Michael *are* getting married. They love each other. And there's not a thing you can do about it."

"Love?" Connor's eyes glittered in the dwindling sunlight and his sharp bark of laughter caused Victoria to bristle defensively. "Is that what women call it?"

"It's what Michael calls it, too." A chill enveloped Victoria. She must be mad to challenge this man. "And what gives you the right to sit judgment on what Michael and Suzy feel for each other, anyway?"

He stared down his nose at her. "Love is overrated."

Hoisting the basket of hymn books to stop them falling, she said, "If you're that cynical then perhaps you shouldn't have agreed to be Michael's best man."

"Victoria—"

"No, Suzy." She broke free of the bride-to-be's restraining arm. "What he said was rude and uncalled for."

Suzy looked decidedly uncomfortable.

"Can I take those for you?" Connor had the basket before she could object.

"Thanks," she said ungraciously.

"It looked like you were about to drop them."

The superior tone annoyed her afresh. Victoria wondered

if the hard, handsome man in front of her had ever apologized to anyone. He would, she vowed. "Are you proud of yourself?"

"For helping relieve you of the basket?" He tilted his head sideways. "I suppose I am."

"That's not what I mean." And he knew it. Splaying her hands on her skinny hips, Victoria faced Connor down. She was taller than Suzy by a head, yet Connor still loomed over her. For a moment her resolve wavered; then she stiffened her spine. "Is that what you wanted?" She nodded to Suzy where she stood, her shoulders sagging. "You're going to ruin her day if you carry on like this."

There was a long, brooding silence.

"Sorry." But he didn't sound sorry in the least.

"That's the best you can do?" demanded Victoria.

"I accept his apology," Suzy said quickly. "I understand why he's upset."

"I'm not *upset*," he growled, and gave Victoria a killing how-dare-you stare before stalking off in Michael's wake, the basket swinging incongruously at his side.

"Jerk!" Victoria fumed. To her astonishment she found that her hands were trembling. She brushed them over her hair, more to regain her composure than to smooth the style. She was too tired to be tactful. "What does Michael see in the man?"

"Make allowances for him." Suzy put a hand on her arm. "His girlfriend just dumped him for his business partner. It can't be a good time for him."

Victoria gave a derisive laugh. "I don't blame her one bit. No sane woman could live with a jerk like him."

"He's hurting," Suzy protested.

"Didn't you hear the way he said 'love'? Like it was something foreign to him. Connor North feels as much emotion as a slab of granite."

"Michael says he doesn't share much, so maybe he did love her. He's been very good about it, even letting her keep the house."

"I'm sure she deserved it."

"Shh." Suzy's grip on her arm tightened. "He might hear you."

"I don't care."

"Well, I do. C'mon, Tory, Michael and I were seriously hoping the two of you would become...well...friends."

Friends with Connor North? Friendship implied affection, warmth and loyalty. Victoria couldn't imagine Rock-Face ever exhibiting any of those qualities. She stared down at the person who knew her better than anyone in the world and gave a snort of disbelief. "You're dreaming, Suz."

Had Michael and Suzy been planning to match-make?

"Okay." Suzy held up her hands. "I'm not going to argue, so let's change the subject. I've been meaning to ask you, Tory, if you wouldn't mind popping past the cottage to water the potted plants while we're on honeymoon. Connor might forget."

Victoria frowned suspiciously. "What do you mean 'Connor might forget?'"

"He's been staying with Michael this past week and the two of them have been working like dogs every evening to get the house all painted inside. And Connor will look after it while we're on honeymoon—Michael dotes on that house."

"I suppose I can drop round in my lunch hour—that way I won't bump into him." Then Victoria clicked her tongue. "Suzy, you're not intending to start off your marriage with a houseguest, are you?"

"Oh, no, he's not the type to be a third wheel—though he's helped Michael heaps with the house. Michael could never have done as much alone. No, Connor will find a place while we're on honeymoon. Michael just felt he needed a few days to get over the shock of losing his woman, his home and his business in one shot."

Victoria steeled herself against a sneaky twinge of sympathy. However hard a time he'd had, it was no reason to attack Suzy. "I'm sure he'll recover."

"Please be nice to him, Tory." Suzy stretched her blue eyes wide. "I don't want the wedding photos ruined because the maid of honor and best man have a fistfight."

No sane woman could live with a jerk like him.

Telling himself that the dislike was mutual didn't stop the maid of honor's words from rankling as Connor marched across the car park tucked away behind the church hall. He came to a stop where Michael Mason rummaged in the trunk of a modest Toyota parked in the dark shade of two tall pines.

"That woman is a menace." Connor dropped the basket filled with hymn books into the trunk next to the black rollaway bag.

The groom's head came up, and the brown eyes of a man Connor met twice weekly for a killer game of squash grew cool as Michael said with deceptive mildness, "Suzy is going to be my wife, Connor. Watch what you say."

Connor did a double take. "Wow. You've got it bad." His mouth slanted as Michael tensed. "Steady on, I was talking about the maid of honor."

"Victoria?" Michael slammed the trunk shut. "She's been friends with Suzy for decades. In fact—"

The sudden gleam in Michael's eyes had Connor bringing his hands up in front of him to ward off the inevitable. "Don't go there—she's not my type."

The woman was way too opinionated.

Michael ignored the warning. "Maybe you need a change from blonds. In fact, Suzy and I thought she might be the perfect antidote to Dana."

Fresh annoyance surged through Connor at the memory of overhearing Suzy telling her friend that he'd been dumped by his girlfriend. And the sympathy in her eyes when she'd said she understood why he was upset.

Upset? Hell, he wasn't upset. He was damned mad.

Mad at Dana. Mad at Paul Harper. Mad at Michael for divulging a confidence. And mad at the irritating, interfering witch who'd forced an apology out of him.

Breathing deeply, he said, "I gather you told Suzy all about Dana?"

Michael extracted a set of car keys from his pants pocket and activated the remote to unlock the doors. "How could I not? She would've found out anyway."

"My business partner and my girlfriend...and I was the last to know." Connor tried to laugh as he went around to the passenger side. "Soap opera stuff, huh?"

The raw hurt and betrayal that two days earlier had scorched all the way to his soul resurfaced. He hated the thought of people picking over the details of his devastated life.

"What Paul did was unforgivable." Michael's mouth was firm as he settled in the seat beside Connor. "And Dana was more than your girlfriend. The woman's been living with you for nearly two years. Hell, you even made her a director of Harper-North."

How Connor regretted Wednesday's drunken bout of self-pity. He'd been away, laying the groundwork to open Harper-North's first Australian office. On his return from Sydney, Dana had hit him with the news that their relationship was over. She had a new lover—the man he'd gone to university with, the man he'd founded a business with. His best friend. His *former* best friend.

Connor had gone to Michael's house, gotten drunk, and blurted it all out. Dumb.

"The whole world shifted on its axis in the three weeks I

was gone." Connor raked his hands through his hair. It needed a cut. The mundane thought steadied him. "Came back to find my life in uproar and you planning marriage." He shook his head. "Crazy."

"Not that crazy. I've know Suzy a while, even though we only started dating about a month ago."

"A month?" Connor raised his brows. "After two years I didn't know what kind of treachery Dana was capable of. You should've taken more time."

"A month. A year. Two years. It's not going to make a difference to how I feel about Suzy."

"So what makes you so sure Suzy isn't after a lifelong meal ticket?"

A chuckle filled the car. "Mate, I'm not the billionaire here. I don't wear thousand-dollar suits—" Michael gave Connor's Armani a mocking inspection "—drive a Maserati, or live in a marble mansion."

"I don't live there anymore."

This week's showdown came back to haunt Connor. Paul had already moved into *his* house with Dana. But he'd wring every cent that he could from the pair of them in exchange for the mansion that Dana had craved…and the share of Harper-North that Connor had walked away from. They weren't going to get off scott-free.

"Sorry." The laughter faded from Michael's eyes. "But trust me, Suzy's not marrying me for money. She's a teacher, just like me, so our incomes are pretty equal."

Dana had been trying to wheedle an engagement ring out of Connor for ages. His thoughts came to a grinding halt. Had Suzy tricked Michael into a proposal with the oldest trick in the book?

"What about children?" Connor prodded. Dana had begged for a child. But Connor had resisted. He hadn't wanted marriage—which he suspected was the real reason for Dana's desperate desire for a child. A child would've been a mistake. They were both too busy for kids, he'd told her.

Michael turned the key in the ignition. His jaw had firmed and his hands gripped the steering wheel.

"I'm not asking if this woman's already pregnant," Connor lied hastily as the motor took. "Just wondering if she views you as a father figure for any children she has." A high school guidance counselor, Michael would make the perfect mark for a solo mother wanting financial and emotional support.

"She doesn't have any." The reply was clipped.

"That's a relief. I was worried she might be a desperate divorcée." Connor paused as they rolled down a narrow lane lined with clipped hedges that hid the church from view.

"She's divorced but she's not desperate." Michael's jaw jutted out, a sign of the stubborn streak that usually remained hidden beneath his affable, calm exterior. "You'll like Suzy, Connor—if you let yourself. There's no catch."

Connor stared at Michael's profile, aware he wasn't getting anywhere. The strange notion that his orderly life had spun out of control increased. He shook his head. "You're not listening. There's always a catch."

"Of course I'm listening."

"But?" Something about the set of Michael's jaw told Connor this was one of the rare times that none of his arguments were going to succeed.

In the years he'd been playing squash with Michael he'd come to value the calm, unconditional friendship they'd forged. Connor often offered Michael financial advice, and only twice had Michael disregarded it. The first time Michael had lost thousands on a development that went belly up. The second time Connor had advised him to steer clear of a derelict Edwardian cottage on a busy road. Michael had wanted to use an unexpected legacy from a great-aunt as a deposit. Connor had warned him the restoration would devour money faster than a hungry loan shark.

But Michael had bought the place anyway and spent every weekend working on it. Connor had taken to dropping by on Sunday afternoons to lend Michael a hand—much to Dana's disgust—and the manual labor involved in stripping old paint-work and restoring the cottage had proved extremely reward-ing. As the house took shape Connor finally admitted he'd been wrong. Despite the exorbitant amount of time and money it consumed, Michael's home was special.

It had reminded him of the days when he and Paul had first started out, fired by dreams of preserving as many forgotten buildings as they could.

When had they lost that idealism? When had it all become about the next million?

Yet just because Michael had been right about that old place of his didn't mean this madly rushed marriage would work out, Connor decided as they waited for a break in the traffic.

"But…Suzy's nothing like Dana."

Connor bristled at the mention of Dana's name. "I never said she was."

Michael threw him a disbelieving look. "Don't let what Dana did embitter you. I think you're well rid of her. I never liked her, you know. You deserve someone better."

"Right now I'm hardly in the mood to play dating games," Connor growled.

"You'll get over it." Michael nosed the Toyota onto the road that ran past the front of the church. "We'll find someone to kiss your broken heart better at the wedding tomorrow."

Connor gave him a baleful glare. "My heart isn't broken."

"No," Michael agreed. "It's your pride that's battered."

"Thanks, mate, I really needed to hear that!"

Michael was still laughing as they pulled up in front of the church gate where the bride and her maid of honor waited.

Despite Suzy's blonde prettiness, Connor found his gaze drawn to her friend. A patina of reserve clung to her. There was not a hint of feminine flounce in the straight black skirt, black stockings or the tailored white shirt. Yet when she moved toward the car, she carried herself with an easy, swinging grace that contrasted sharply with her coolly composed features.

"Best therapy right now would be another woman. Victoria—"

"No." Connor looked away from the termagant and directed a stony stare at Michael. "I definitely don't need another hard-boiled career woman with her eye on the main chance. So don't try any matchmaking tonight or you'll be looking for a new best man for your wedding tomorrow."

Two

Connor barely noticed the radiant beauty of the stained-glass window backlit by the afternoon sun. Or how the kaleidoscopic light fell onto the faces of bride and groom, giving them an otherworldly quality. Instead he stood stiffly next to *her* behind the bridal pair as they exchanged vows, Michael's voice deep and serious, Suzy sounding much breathier.

His anger at *her* had driven away his annoyance that Michael had dared to discuss Connor's abortive personal affairs with Suzy. He couldn't bear the thought of being pitied by anyone.

Although he could hardly accuse *her* of pitying him.

Unwillingly Connor slanted a sideways look at the maid of honor. He'd planned to ignore her today. She'd said little at dinner last night. Despite his threats to Michael, his and Suzy's matchmaking efforts had been irritatingly obvious, and Connor had no intention of giving the argumentative woman any encouragement. The next woman he dated would be pure entertainment…no strings and plenty of hot sex. Not another high-flyer married to her career.

Her pallor last night had suggested she'd be more prone to headaches than hot sex. So had her attitude—she'd excused herself just after eleven, pleading exhaustion, but when he'd offered her a ride home she'd given him a look that suggested she'd rather eat slugs, and insisted on calling a taxi.

He had to admit she looked much better today. Suzy's doing, no doubt. He almost hadn't recognized her at the church door. Only her height—she was tall, her head coming up to his chin—her slender body and those wary hazel eyes had identified her.

Yet she was impossible to ignore.

Yesterday's rumpled white shirt and black sacklike skirt had given way to an ultrafeminine dress of some pale, gauzy fabric that turned what he could see of her skin to the delicious luminescence of pearl. She'd done something different with her hair, too, twisting the dark strands up so it exposed the soft, pale skin of her neck, and a couple of loose tendrils brushed the slope of her shoulders.

And all that bare, feminine skin tempted him to touch, to stroke.

What the hell was he thinking? One week without a woman to call his own and even this plain, uptight female was starting to look attractive.

Despite Michael's advice, the last thing he needed in his life was a woman. Even if he did, this one didn't qualify—she was way too intense. And, as Suzy's best friend, too complicated.

A hush fell over the church and he turned his head to watch Michael slip a plain gold band onto Suzy's finger. There was a moment where the world seemed to hold its breath, and Michael looked positively bewitched.

Connor let out the breath he was holding.

He should've advised Michael on the wedding band. Women

liked diamonds. Dana would've demanded a humdinger—for investment purposes of course. Michael should at least have had a row of diamonds channel set.

The priest was giving Michael permission to kiss the bride. Connor blanked out the sighs from the congregation and his awareness of the woman standing beside him, and found himself hoping Suzy would be more trustworthy than Dana had been.

Then, thankfully, the service was over. As they filed out of the church Connor pulled out his BlackBerry and made a note to himself about a meeting with a Realtor to look at new offices that he'd remembered he was supposed to attend on Monday.

The maid of honor—he really should remember her name—was glaring at him. Guiltily he stuck the BlackBerry back in his pocket.

"Wait," she ordered as he headed for the stairs. "Michael and Suzy will want a photo at the church door."

Violet? Was that her name? "There's a wedding photographer to do that." He gestured to where the man stood. "I didn't bring a camera."

"They might want us to be in the photo with them. We should smile. Look happy."

"Sure."

She shot him a narrow look; clearly she hadn't missed his sarcasm. Not Violet, but it had been something equally old-fashioned. Edith? No, that wasn't right, either.

He was saved from the need to reply by Michael and Suzy's emergence from the church, their faces alight with what even he could recognize was joy. Envy speared him. Then he suppressed it. He was done with love and romance… from now on his relationships would be based purely on sex. No emotion. No tenderness.

That way there would be no betrayal.

The bridal couple paused under the arched church door

beneath a flurry of pink-and-white rose petals, and the photographer leapt into action.

The damn woman had been right.

Unbidden, his eyes landed on her. She was smiling, and Connor had to admit it transformed her face. At least she wasn't gloating. His gaze lingered on her curved lips and he couldn't help noticing that her mouth was very pretty when it wasn't screwed up in disapproval.

"Connor, Victoria, over here!" called Suzy.

Victoria. Of course! "We're being summoned." He placed a hand under her elbow. Her skin was silky beneath his fingertips. Out of nowhere a totally unexpected surge of lust hit him. Perhaps the wedding reception wouldn't be such an ordeal after all…

Suzy was beckoning impatiently. "Come on, we need a photo with the two of you."

"I told you so," muttered Victoria.

Connor shot her a look of dislike. Okay, so he'd been wrong on two counts. Firstly, the reception was going to be every bit as bad as he'd imagined and, secondly, she *had* been gloating. She'd simply concealed it under that sweetly deceptive smile.

All desire waned. It didn't need Michael's grin—nor the pointed look to Connor's hand where it rested—for his hand to drop away from her arm.

The further he stayed away from Queen we-are-not-amused Victoria, the better.

On entering the ballroom, Connor discovered—much to his horror—that rather than the two of them flanking the bridal pair, he and Victoria had been seated beside each other.

"Give the two of you a chance to talk, seeing that all my attention will be on my bride," Michael murmured sotto voce, holding a chair out for Suzy, who glanced up and gave Connor a little wave, her eyes glittering with mischief.

Irritation swarmed through Connor and he glared at the smug groom.

Connor survived the first round of speeches by ignoring Victoria completely, although if he'd been honest he'd have had to admit that the subtly seductive scent she wore didn't make that easy. By the time he had to propose a toast to the bride and groom he'd downed three glasses of too-sweet wedding wine. When the first notes of the wedding waltz struck up he looked vainly around for a waiter to order a double whiskey.

"Come on," an unwelcome voice beside him prompted. "We should join them."

"I'm not dancing," he said flatly, settling for another glass of sweet champagne with a grimace.

Her gaze landed on the glass and her straight eyebrows drew together in a frown. "Surely you're not going to use Suzy and Michael's wedding as an excuse to get drunk?"

Deliberately provocative, he raised the tulip-glass in a mocking toast. "I'm celebrating the love that you believe in."

"Don't be so flippant." Her disapproval deepened. "This is the happiest day of Suzy and Michael's life and you're going to ruin it for them if you carry on. And all because you're too busy feeling sorry for yourself."

Connor blinked in disbelief. "*What* did you say?" He couldn't have heard right. Everyone had been pussyfooting around the subject of Dana and Paul's affair. Surely she wouldn't dare...

Their eyes locked. Hers were more green than brown, flashing little flecks of gold. It wasn't pity he read there but disdain.

He'd heard perfectly. And grew convinced this woman would dare anything.

Anger knotted in his chest.

"Snap out of it. Think of someone except yourself for a

change. It's only a couple more hours." Her gaze dropped to the glass in front of him. "And I suggest you slow down on the alcohol."

"I don't know who you think you are—" he lowered his voice to a lethal rasp "—but you are way out of line."

"I'm Victoria." A grim smile accompanied the words. "In case you've forgotten, I'm the bride's best friend—" she emphasized *best* "—but I don't understand how Michael can call you a friend at all. I certainly haven't seen you do anything to deserve it."

Her words stung. He was on his feet before he could think. "I don't have to listen to this!"

Startled dismay flitted across her face. She cast a quick glance to where the bride was nestled in the groom's arms. Michael chose that moment to glance at them over the top of Suzy's curls. Victoria muttered something that sounded suspiciously like an expletive, pushed her chair back and grabbed his hand.

"Great." The beaming smile she turned on him transformed her face. "Let's get dancing."

Connor stared at her, poleaxed by the wattage of her smile. It made her look almost beautiful.

He blurted out, "You should smile more often," and in a daze followed her onto the dance floor.

Michael slowed to a shuffle and mouthed, "Everything okay?"

Crap, she was right. Again. He *was* being selfish. Forcing a smile, Connor gave Michael the thumbs-up.

Everything was great.

Right.

Somehow the maid of honor was in his arms, swaying into the wedding waltz, her dress soft and silky under the hands he hadn't even realized he'd placed on her waist.

"How did you meet Michael?" she asked, still smiling up at him.

He again noticed how lovely her mouth was and forgot the sheer fury she aroused in him. It was, after all, a very distracting mouth. One taste…it would surely rid his tongue of the aftertaste of that awful champagne.

"We're members of the same squash club. When our original partners stopped playing—" Paul had preferred the gym "—we were both at a loose end, so we teamed up." That had been six years ago. Despite seeing his business partner every day of his life, Connor realized Michael had proved to be the better friend. He switched off that train of thought before the bleakness that had hovered over him for the past three days descended again.

No Paul or Dana today.

Not even dreaming up grisly plans for revenge.

"Do you work with Suzy?" he asked, determined to get his mind out of the rut it kept drifting back to. Maybe Michael was right and a date with Victoria would be a good distraction.

The smile faded and her eyes turned cool. "I'm an accountant—Michael told you that, remember?"

"That's right." No, a date with Victoria would be a very bad idea. "But should you have reminded me? Isn't that rude?" He gave her a sharklike smile that held no humor.

"Not as impolite as your evident disinterest—you can't even remember my name."

Touché. He took in the flare of rosy color on her cheeks, the sparkle of spirit in her eyes. How had he ever thought she was dreary? "Your name is Victoria. And I can't think why I thought you were a teacher."

"Perhaps because I know Suzy?"

No, it was that silent reserve, and the way she didn't hesitate to correct him. He wasn't accustomed to that—except from his assistant Iris. And that was different; Iris was a friend of his mother's and had known him for three decades.

"It's the way you told me off."

She slanted him an upward glance. "Yesterday or just now? Either way, you deserved it."

Connor tried to convince himself that yesterday's scene had been her fault, but he couldn't shrug off the discomfort that lingered at the memory of the expression in Suzy's eyes. Telling himself that *Victoria* had provoked him didn't wash. He was accountable for his own actions, and the fact that his life was in chaos was irrelevant.

Instead of responding, he simply shrugged.

"I think you need people to stand up to you more often."

She pursed that luscious mouth again and Connor had a wild desire to shake her out of her righteous complacency.

"Everyone seems to know what I need." Her lips parted and Connor got the impression she, too, was about to tell him exactly what she thought he needed. Wickedly determined to silence her, he drew her closer into his arms, bent his head and murmured in her ear, "Michael thinks I need a woman."

Alone with Suzy in the hotel's honeymoon suite where they'd retreated to mend the flounce of Suzy's wedding dress, Victoria couldn't forget the heady excitement that dancing with Connor had aroused—or the words he'd whispered in her ear.

Michael thinks I need a woman.

His touch on her waist…the way he made her feel so fragile and feminine in his arms…the glorious male scent of him that had surrounded her. She shivered.

Heavens, it had been too long since she'd dated if a man she despised could reduce her to quivering desire, she decided acerbically. Victoria pulled the final stitch tight and savagely snapped off the thread. "There, that should hold as long as you don't put a heel through the hem again."

"Victoria, I need a favor."

Glancing up from where she knelt beside Suzy, Victoria

met Suzy's eyes in the floor-to-ceiling mirrored closet doors. "What's the favor?"

"Don't feel you have to agree."

"How bad can it be? Come on, spit it out."

There was a pause as Victoria arranged the skirts around Suzy's legs, waiting. Then, "It's harder than I thought it would be."

At the hesitant note in Suzy's voice, Victoria's attention sharpened. She rocked back on her heels—no easy task given the close-fitting sheath dress she'd chosen to wear. "You can ask me anything—you know that."

"This is different…it's difficult. And I'm going to swear you to secrecy if you agree. You can never, ever tell anyone about it."

Curiouser and curiouser. "Can it be more difficult than asking me to tell your mother you'd driven over her rose-bushes? Did I refuse then?" Victoria raised an eyebrow, inviting Suzy to smile with her. "Granted, you didn't swear me to secrecy that time."

But Suzy didn't laugh.

"You can't be having second thoughts about your wedding?" Victoria's heart sank at the thought. "You're not about to run out on Michael, are you?"

Suzy's blue eyes grew round. "Oh, no! I'd never do that. How could you even think that, Tory? Michael's everything I ever dreamed of finding."

The certainty in Suzy's voice caused a sudden flare of envy. Pushing herself up off the carpet, Victoria suppressed it. She'd made her choices. After a string of disastrous relationships had ended in accusations that she was too ambitious, she'd decided there were more rewarding ways to fill her life.

She had her job. A fantastic job where she'd built up an impressive client list. And she had Suzy, the best and most loyal friend anyone could wish for.

She didn't need a man…or a wedding.

So why on earth was she envying Suzy?

And realistically what chance did she have of finding the kind of man she wanted? A man who would let her keep the independence she craved, and love her for it? The memory of a pair of hard hands at her waist, a harsh whisper in her ear, stole over her. Certainly not a man like Connor North. Arrogant. Demanding. A man who didn't even believe in love.

Drawing a shaky breath, Victoria forced herself to focus on Suzy, on the issue at hand rather than on the illusion of finding someone who would love her forever. "I just thought you might've belatedly remembered your vow never to marry again."

"That was years ago." Suzy waved a dismissive hand and turned to the mirror to study herself. "I'd just come from the lawyer's office and a horrible fight about the divorce settlement with Thomas. Of course I was feeling a little sore about marriage."

A *little* sore? Victoria almost laughed at the understatement but the tension in her friend's shoulders warned against it. Suzy had studiously avoided weddings for a year after that first disastrous attempt at matrimony.

"I love Michael. I want…*need*…this time to work." Suzy spun back, her dress whirling around in a froth of white, and slanted Victoria an imploring look. "You of all people must know that I want what Mum and Dad had."

How had Suzy unerringly known to pick on the one thing that would silence Victoria?

Suzy's parents had adored each other—and they'd been loving and incredibly kind. Whenever Victoria's father had been overcome by a bout of wanderlust, her mother had retreated into a sobbing self-pity. It had been Suzy's parents who had offered Victoria a bed for the night, cooked meals for her and ensured that she made it to school with her clothes clean and her homework done.

When they'd drowned in a boating accident, Suzy and Victoria had been at university and Victoria felt the double loss almost as acutely as her friend. She would never forget the sanctuary that Suzy's home had become during her adolescent years. It had saved her, creating a debt she could never repay. Without Suzy and her parents, who knew how she would've turned out?

Victoria held her best friend's gaze. "I hope you find the same happiness your parents had. I think it's wonderful that you've found someone—I just don't want you to be hurt again."

Suzy threw her arms around Victoria. "Relax, Michael is nothing like Thomas."

Clumsily hugging Suzy back, Victoria stared over her friend's shoulder at their reflection in the mirror, Suzy so beautiful in her high-necked lacy wedding gown, the hem no longer dragging on the ground.

She wanted Suzy to stay happy forever. She'd hated how Thomas had made bright, bubbly Suzy so miserable. Just like her own father had killed all the joy in her mother…

How she'd resented her mother for allowing it. How she'd wished that her mother had stood up and told her father to leave, never to return—and to stop neglecting them both—rather than weeping pathetically and sinking into depression every time he vanished. If only her mother had been stronger, not so emotionally dependent on the handsome but feckless man she'd married.

Suzy's arms dropped away. "Stop frowning, Tory. It's my wedding day, remember?"

Victoria blinked. "How could I forget?" she said wryly, gesturing to their reflections in the mirror. "Your gorgeous dress…the flowers…the suite."

"Connor arranged the suite—and our honeymoon to Hawaii. It's his wedding present to us. Wasn't that generous?"

Victoria had no intention of acknowledging any redeeming

qualities in the man. "All this talk of secrets had me concerned. But if you're truly happy then I have no cause to worry."

There was an expression in Suzy's eyes that Victoria had never seen before. A mixture of trepidation and yearning. The sinking feeling returned. "There is something! What is it, Suz? Are you in trouble?"

"Michael knows the reason my marriage to Thomas fell apart was because I couldn't—" Suzy swallowed visibly "—have a baby."

"Oh, Suzy." Victoria took Suzy's hands in hers. Despite the heating in the honeymoon suite, her friend's fingers were cold.

"He knows that Thomas and I tried IVF and that it was unsuccessful. So we talked to a specialist. From my medical records, she thinks there's still a chance I could get pregnant."

"That's wonderful!"

"But only if we can find an egg donor," Suzy finished in a rush, pulling her hands free and, after a quick glance at Victoria, turning away to retrieve her bridal bouquet off the bed behind them.

"You want me to be your donor?" For a moment Victoria wondered what would be involved. Pain. Expense. All sorts of stuff she'd never had to contemplate before. Victoria took in Suzy's tense figure, the way she hunched over her wedding bouquet as she waited for Victoria's reply. What was some physical discomfort compared to Suzy's pain? Suzy had already lost one husband because of her inability to conceive, and while Michael loved her, it would be understandable that she feared his love would diminish as time passed and other couples they knew started to conceive.

Suzy was more than a friend. She was the sister Victoria had never had. Her only family. The person she owed more than she could ever give back. "Of course I'll do it. Consider it a gift. My wedding gift to you and Michael." To help this marriage hold together. To bring Suzy the happiness she richly deserved.

Instantly she was enfolded in a fierce hug, and the fragrance from the posy of white roses and gardenias Suzy clutched wafted around them.

"Thank you!" Suzy's eyes brimmed with tears as she pulled back. "That's the best gift ever…even if it doesn't work out and there's no baby, I'll never forget this."

"Miracles have been known to happen. And no one deserves this miracle more than you, Suz." Victoria felt her own throat clogging up. "Help, now you're making me cry."

Suzy gave her a radiant smile. "It's okay to cry at weddings—so long as it's the happy kind of crying. Now let's get back downstairs—I intend to dance the night away."

Connor wasn't at the wedding table.

Michael thinks I need a woman. Victoria couldn't get his mocking words out of her head. Maybe he'd decided to follow the groom's advice and find a willing female. There would be no shortage of them among the guests.

Searching the dance floor, Victoria couldn't pick out his dark hair and tall figure, which should have towered above everyone else. She drifted around the edge of the polished wooden floor and finally spotted him standing near the open glass doors that led out onto a wide veranda.

He turned his head as if he knew she was watching him and met her gaze. Without a word, he headed for the doors and Victoria followed automatically, drawn against all good sense.

"So do you want to dance out here in the starlight?" He stood in the shadows of the balcony, leaning against the railing, moonlight casting a strange silver-and-black glow over his face.

Her breath caught in her throat. The music spilled through the doors, a slow, sweet, seductive beat. It would take only two steps to bring her into his arms, to feel the heat of his body close to hers again. No. Madness! "The moon's too bright tonight to speak of starlight."

His white teeth glittered as he grinned. "You're probably right—but then I'm sure you make a career of being right."

He pushed away from the railing and moved toward her. "So do you concur with Michael, that the warmth of a woman's body is what I need?" The words cut through the night.

Victoria swallowed, her mouth suddenly dry. Why hadn't she just minded her own business? He wasn't the kind of man to play with.

"If you don't want to dance, what are you looking for? Are you here to offer yourself?" he murmured huskily. "It's supposed to be one of the delights of being the best man, hooking up with the maid of honor. What fun."

Victoria found nothing amusing in his biting tone. "No." She backed up but, before she could retreat, his arms came around her and he lowered his head.

"Don't—" she managed, and then his mouth ground down on hers.

It wasn't a gentle kiss. Full of whiskey and force and anger, it was unlike anything she'd ever experienced.

Victoria struggled but his grip was tight, pinning her arms at her sides. He moved closer, his thighs thrusting against her softness, making it clear he was aroused.

God.

She fought herself free. "What the hell was that about?"

"I don't like being manipulated." He was breathing hard. "I don't want a woman, understand?"

"You're insane." She resisted the urge to retort that he was fooling himself—he was desperate for a woman. For her.

"You're saying you didn't come out for exactly that? Conspiring with your friend, hoping to catch me on the rebound?"

"You are such a jerk." She swung her back on him, determined to leave him out here alone.

He grabbed her and yanked her back. "Not nice."

This time when his lips descended she knew what was coming—and tensed.

But it was different.

Soft, seductive. His tongue stroked the corners of her mouth until she parted her lips, granting him access. This time he kissed her with a dark desire that stirred wants that had never been woken. Dark, traitorous desires. And when his hands swept up over her arms, down her back, she edged closer, craving more—wishing he'd sweep her off to someplace private where they could spend hours together exploring naked skin and sweet sensations.

By the time he ended the kiss she was ready to do whatever he asked.

Connor North set her away from him with shaking hands. "Now, tell me that wasn't what you wanted."

She lifted a hand to her mouth, the fullness of her lips tingling. Damn Connor North. He must surely be aware of his effect on her. Sucking in a shuddering breath, she said, "Don't try it again or I'll slap you so hard it'll leave marks on your face."

He laughed. "Here—" he thrust a pristine, folded white handkerchief at her "—use this for that other dramatic gesture B-grade girls love. Wipe it across your mouth and make the necessary sounds of disgust." His eyes glittered wildly in the half light.

Ignoring the shaky feeling inside, Victoria quirked one expressive, dark eyebrow. "Girls do that to you often?"

"No…but then the women I know don't threaten to slap me, either." His not-so-subtle emphasis of the word *women* caused color to flame in her face.

She balled the handkerchief in a fist, and he flinched as she raised it to his mouth.

"Stand still." Her voice was tight. "Better I wipe my lipstick off *your* mouth."

The curves of his mouth felt full and sensual under the fabric. "There, I'm done."

Connor stared down at the red stain on the white cloth and his lips twisted. "You should have left your mark on my mouth."

He raised his head and Victoria felt the force of his reckless attraction hit her like a surge of current. "Why would I want to do that?" She injected scorn into her voice.

He shrugged carelessly. "It would have given all the gossips something to talk about other than my scurrilous split from Dana."

"I don't want to be linked to you." Victoria was appalled at the idea. "So we're going to go back to the table and smile like crazy—for Suzy and Michael's sake. But after today I intend to take great pains to keep as far away from you as possible."

"That won't be necessary. You're hardly my type..." he paused, then added tauntingly "...Elizabeth."

Victoria spun away and stalked inside and quite spoilt the moment by failing to remind him that her name was Victoria.

Three

Late on Monday afternoon, Connor walked out of the morgue in the small Northland town where the bodies had been taken and gulped in a lungful of crisp, fresh air. *Michael.* The face he'd known so well in life had been unrecognizable in death. And all the dazzling laughter had left Suzy forever. Connor craved the deep, cleansing peace of tears.

But grown men didn't cry.

Nor did he have time to grieve. Picking up his pace, he jogged across the car park to where the Maserati waited.

But once inside, he sat motionless, staring blindly through the windshield.

He should call Victoria. The thought came from nowhere. He sighed. What the hell was the purpose? Except to upset her further.

Pulling out of the car park, he headed for the highway.

Not far from the exit to the town he saw again the sickening skid marks, and the white symbols the police had painted on the tarmac.

Driven by a nameless, senseless urge Connor pulled over and got out.

The grass verge was peppered with glass, and he stepped over the deep furrows Michael's tires had gouged out of the turf. A light country breeze blew across his face and cars whizzed past. There was none of the sense that Michael's spirit still lingered—as Connor realized he'd hoped for when he'd pulled over.

It's not fair. They should be here! Victoria's words rang in his ears.

Balling his fists against his eyes, he faced the fact that he would never again see the slight smile that changed Michael's expression from intellectual to human. He would never again play squash against that killer competitive drive that few people knew Michael possessed.

A tidal wave of sorrow swept over him, and a moment later the aftershock of loneliness set in, paralyzing him.

Even after the fiasco with his ex-girlfriend and his business partner, he'd been able to act. He hadn't even missed Dana— he'd kept himself too busy. Working like a fiend to get the Phoenix Corporation up. Going to the gym. Squash and beers with Michael. Dating a string of women who entertained but didn't enthrall. While all the time Michael watched him with that quiet smile and offered advice that Connor hadn't taken.

And now he'd never see Michael again.

Even fighting with Victoria had to be better than this miserable emptiness. Then he remembered her face as he'd last seen it yesterday. Devastated by the loss of Suzy. Again the compulsion to call Victoria nagged him.

Michael…

Hell.

He dropped his balled fists to his side, blinked rapidly and swallowed, furious at the hot tightness in his chest. Never was a long time. And right now it stretched before him endlessly.

He wasn't accustomed to being powerless.

The only things left for him to do for Michael were so final—so futile. Arranging the funeral. Carrying the coffin. Executing his will. Ensuring that Dylan was protected.

A car swept by in a rush of air, the driver hooting, jerking him out of his trance of grief.

Dylan.

Connor raked both his hands through his wind-ruffled hair. Michael had loved Dylan; he loved Dylan, too.

No doubt about it, Dylan was special. Never had a baby been more loved. And that's the way it had always been meant to be.

When, shortly after his wedding, Michael had confessed to Connor that he was sterile as a result of contracting mumps as a boy, Connor had agreed to donate sperm to allow the Masons a chance at a baby. It hadn't been a hard decision for him to make. Anyone who knew Suzy and Michael could see that they were made to be parents. Perfect parents. Yet they'd worried about how their baby might one day react if he discovered Conner was his biological father.

Michael and Suzy had wanted the truth about his biological father to stay forever secret—and Connor had acquiesced to their request. The baby had always been intended to be theirs. Not his.

But now Michael and Suzy were dead.

Connor flinched at the finality of the word. But he would not break his vow to the Masons. At least not until Dylan was old enough to understand why he'd been created from his father's friend's seed.

The foggy lethargy that had clung to him for most of the day started to lift. Connor strode back to the Maserati.

At last he had something to do. Something worthwhile. He

had a duty—one he would not fail in. He would bring Dylan up to remember the fine man that Michael had been. And someday, when Dylan was older, he would explain how much his parents had loved him—and wanted him. That would be the time to tell Dylan—and the world—the truth.

Victoria reached for the shrilling phone and Dylan's eyes, which had been growing heavier, popped open. He again started to suck greedily on the bottle she'd been feeding him.

Juggling the handset and the bottle, she waited for him to settle again in the crook of her arm before saying, "Hello?"

"I'll be there in under an hour."

Her heart started to knock against her ribs. "Who is this speaking, please?"

"Don't play games, Victoria," growled Connor. "It's been a hell of a day."

Victoria fell silent. Her day had been pretty awful, too. First thing this morning she'd called Bridget Edge, the managing partner at work, to let her know she wouldn't be in, that she was taking compassionate leave because her best friend had died.

There had been a short silence. Then, after uttering per-functory condolences, Bridget had asked when she would be back at work.

Victoria had known in that moment it wouldn't be wise to say anything about Dylan. Yet.

Bridget would never understand. She wasn't married and had no children. How could Victoria have confessed that Dylan needed her right now? Or that she needed Dylan more than anything in the world? Bridget would've thought she'd lost her marbles. Finally Victoria said she would be back as soon as the funeral had been held.

Suzy had placed Dylan in a day care center a month ago. So far he'd only been going for half a day as Suzy eased herself back into teaching part-time. But if Dylan returned, it would save her from needing to make other arrangements— and keep his routine normal. Tomorrow she'd call the supervisor, let her know to expect Dylan back.

Tomorrow—when she'd gotten a handle on her grief and could talk without her throat tightening up.

Oh, Suzy!

She certainly didn't feel like facing Connor in less than an hour. Her emotions were too raw, her heart too sore. "I've just gotten Dylan to sleep and I'm about to take a bath. Perhaps we can talk tomorrow?"

"I thought you might want a copy of Michael and Suzy's will."

"Michael and Suzy's will?" Good grief, she hadn't even given a thought to a will. Most unlike her. Her gaze dropped to Dylan, whose mouth was now just twitching on the teat. Emotion overwhelmed her in a hot, poignant wave. The baby had kept her mercifully busy most of the day. He'd been querulous, almost as if he knew....

Except that wasn't possible.

Connor was speaking again. She forced herself to concentrate.

"Yes, a joint will. I've just dropped the original at my solicitor's so they can start winding up the estate."

"I could've done that. It's not going to be a complicated estate."

"You're too busy. Besides I'm the executor."

Hurt blasted her. She'd been the executor of Suzy's will before Suzy had gotten married.

Dylan grunted uneasily.

Cuddling the baby closer, she rocked him in a slow rhythm. "I didn't know Suzy and Michael had a joint will."

She'd nagged Suzy a couple of times to update her will when she was pregnant, but after Dylan was born, Victoria had forgotten all about it in the hectic pace of everyday work. That would have been around the time she'd taken over two new, big accounts on top of her already crippling workload. She'd finally built the practice she'd always wanted, but not without sacrifice.

"My solicitor updated it for them about a year ago." Connor's voice was clipped. "There's not a great deal in the estate."

"They both worked for state schools. They had expenses...." Victoria broke off, then added lamely, "And debts." She'd promised never to reveal her part in Dylan's conception. It certainly wasn't for her to reveal the staggering costs involved—she'd contributed a large sum despite Suzy and Michael's resistance.

"Not surprising," Connor concurred, "given they had a mortgage, too. But Michael took out life insurance to cover that."

Victoria knew Connor had spent hours helping Michael renovate the Masons's home. He'd even organized grants from a historic trust for assistance.

A sense of guilt filled her. Connor had clearly sorted out Michael's money matters, whereas she, an accountant, had failed to protect Dylan and Suzy's interests, leaving it to her new husband to look after her. And would his life insurance cover the IVF debts?

I'll make it up to you, Dylan.

She stroked the baby's soft head. He would want for nothing that was in her power to give him.

She'd contributed to Dylan's coming into the world, given Michael and Suzy the precious eggs they'd needed.

Dylan was a part of her.

"Are you still there?" The impatience in Connor's voice jerked her back.

"Yes. I was just thinking." The baby had just fallen asleep with the suddenness that still took Victoria by surprise. "Once the estate's been wound up I can invest the proceeds for Dylan."

There was a deafening silence.

Then Connor said, "I've always looked after Michael's business affairs."

And she'd always helped Suzy. Except when she'd become too busy. Discomfort filled Victoria.

This was not a time for a power struggle. She had to do her best to accommodate Connor; already he'd done a better job of looking after Suzy—and Dylan—when she'd been remiss.

But it will never happen again, she silently promised the baby in her arms. She was nothing like her parents. She would never neglect Dylan.

"Connor, as executor of the estate, of course you'd need to approve the investments. I'm sure we'll be able to work together in Dylan's best interests." She might not like him but they were both grown adults.

"I'm sure we will." Connor didn't sound nearly as convinced. "As Dylan's—" he broke off "—*guardian* you can bet your bottom dollar I will be very interested."

Her heart stopped. "Guardian?" she croaked. Her mind raced. Had Michael decided to appoint Connor North the baby's guardian? "*You* are Dylan's guardian?" Oh, Suzy, how could you let this happen?

Connor's voice, terse and cool, came over the line. "That's what I want to talk to you about. I'll be there in half an hour."

By the time Connor arrived, Victoria had laid Dylan down in his traveling cot, showered and changed into a simple long-sleeved dress, and had just poured herself a cup of tea.

Rushing across the living room to open the front door before Connor could ring the doorbell, she pressed her finger to her lips and motioned him into the kitchen. "I just got him to sleep."

In the kitchen, Victoria honed in on the subject that had

been eating at her since their telephone conversation. "I'd like to see the will." She did her best to keep the hostility out of her voice, to keep it level and professional.

Connor drew a leather document holder from under his arm and eyed the counter, which was covered with dirty dishes.

Embarrassment spread through Victoria. But then he hadn't been looking after a baby all day.

A surreptitious glance revealed lines of tiredness etched deep into his face, though they failed to mute the impact of his hard, handsome features.

Only the loosened tie and undone top button of his white shirt hinted at the turmoil he must be going through.

The will could wait—whatever it held would not change now. And Connor looked like a train wreck.

"Would you like a cup of coffee?"

"God, I don't know if I need more stimulants," Connor muttered, leaning against the counter.

She gestured to the crowded countertop. "I've just made tea for myself. Would you like a cup?"

She took his grunt as assent, poured him a cup of tea from the little white teapot and topped the brew up with boiling water.

He glared into the cup she passed him. "What the hell is this?"

"Chamomile tea," she said sweetly. "Lots of antioxidants. Good for you in times of stress."

"I doubt it will help." His startlingly pale eyes clashed with hers but the opacity in them caused Victoria's heart to bump and her throat to contract with painful emotion. She wanted to offer him the same comfort she craved—an embrace that went beyond words—but she knew he wouldn't accept it. Not from her.

And to be truthful she didn't care much for him, either. But she felt empathy for him—in the same way she felt pity for herself. She'd lost the person she'd been most deeply bonded to in the world. And, hard as it was to imagine Rock-Man bonded to anyone, Michael had been fond of him. Judging by the emptiness in Connor's eyes, somewhere in that cold heart he'd been fond of Michael, too.

The sadness—the futility of it all—made her want to weep.

But she couldn't let herself forget that he was Dylan's guardian now. Please God, he hadn't been granted custody, too.

Connor wasn't the right person to bring up Dylan—he was too hard. Yet, given the animosity between them, it would be no easy task convincing him *she* was the right person. But failure to do so was not an option.

Because even though she hadn't carried him in her womb, Dylan had been conceived from her egg—he was her baby.

"Come and sit out here." Picking up the two cups and saucers she led him to the small deck that opened off the living room, edged with planter boxes filled with primulas and purple pansies.

Without a word, Connor followed.

Once seated, he placed the leather document holder on the white wrought-iron table where she often ate breakfast, and zipped it open.

Unable to restrain herself, Victoria snatched up the will, scanning the headings as she flicked through the pages. And found the clause that spelled out guardianship and custody.

Four

Fury bubbled up inside Victoria. She threw the papers down on the table and her chair scraped back against the deck. "You told me you were Dylan's guardian," she accused.

"Coguardian." Connor shrugged. "And we share custody, too. We need to discuss it."

The coldhearted bastard had nearly given her heart failure. She'd thought she'd have to *beg* to be allowed a say in Dylan's upbringing. All her unspoken reservations about her ability to be the kind of mother that Dylan needed came crashing in on her.

A gust of chilly wind cut through the fabric of her dress. She shivered. Crossing her arms, she rubbed her hands absently up and down her body. She couldn't allow her insecurities to take hold. She had to believe in herself. Because she was the only parent Dylan had.

Joint custody and coguardianship. How on earth was that going to work? Damn, what had Suzy been thinking?

Or not thinking.

Clearly Suzy had not imagined dying. Suzy would not have thought how impractical it all was to juggle such a young baby between two households.

Sure, it had been done before. But Connor had no motive to cooperate—it wasn't as if he was the baby's father. Still, as a single man who ran a large business, he probably wouldn't want to be hamstrung with a baby. Her heart lifted a little at the realization. In fact, he'd be glad to be rid of the burden.

Connor moved his chair a little nearer and Victoria tensed as she always did when he invaded her space. He stopped, too close now, and leaned toward her. Protectively she tightened her arms around herself. She could smell the crisp, lemony scent of his aftershave, which still lingered after the long day.

The light-gray eyes held her captive. "Victoria, if you don't mind keeping Dylan for another day or so while I get a room ready and painted out for him, I'll take him as soon as I can. Certainly by Thursday."

The spell snapped. Don't mind keeping Dylan? Then give him up to Connor in a day or two? That wasn't happening!

Pushing her chair back, she leapt to her feet. "Dylan will live with me," she cut in, desperate to get this settled as quickly as possible.

"With you?" Connor tilted his head back and gave her a raking glance. He looked unnervingly assured. "No way!"

"What do you mean, no way?" For one awful moment she thought he'd seen all the way to her soul. Read her doubts about her mothering abilities. Then she pulled herself together. She would learn. She would ask the caregivers at the day-care center a thousand questions. There was no way she could do a worse job than her own parents. "How will you cope with a baby? You don't even have a home!" At the blaze of fury in his eyes Victoria wished she'd left the last rash bit unsaid. Heck, she didn't even know if it was still true. "I mean, your ex took your home."

"And I bought another," he said very softly, his eyes glinting dangerously.

So he thought a home could simply be bought?

Something of her skepticism must have shown, because he added, "I have a house with a garden to play ball in and a swimming pool to splash around in—not a shoebox like this." Connor cast a disparaging look around the small deck, his gaze pointedly resting on the pale-cream couches and white carpets visible through the glass sliders. "At least Dylan will be able to grow up a boy in my home. What kind of life would he have here?"

"I'll buy a suburban house with a garden," she said, thinking back to the warmth and love that had filled Suzy's parents' home. "I haven't needed more than this until now."

She could afford to do it. Her savings were in a healthy state. Despite the lump sum she'd insisted on giving Suzy to help with the IVF expenses, which had been worth every cent. The outcome had been Dylan.

"And that'll mean your commute to work will increase." He gave her that sharklike smile. "Or did you intend to stop working?"

"Of course not!"

She needed to carry on working, otherwise how would she be able to give Dylan everything he deserved? Good day care and private schooling were expensive. And Dylan would get the best. She had no intention of leaving Dylan to the mercy of her own ignorance. And besides, it wasn't only for Dylan. She loved her job. It gave her a sense of self-worth. And it paid pretty damn well, too. She couldn't imagine giving up the client base she'd worked so hard to build. Nor would she ever throw away the independence she'd strived all her adult life to secure.

"Don't try telling me you would give up work if Dylan lived with you," she challenged, "because I won't swallow it."

"But I can take as much time off as I want to spend with

Dylan—I'm the boss. And I have a full-time housekeeper. Dylan would be well cared for. It has nothing to do with double standards." His bleak gaze settled on her. "Unlike you, I can devote as much time to Dylan as he needs."

The emptiness that lay behind his eyes was the very reason she could *never* surrender Dylan into his care. He would never be able to convince her he could give Dylan more love than she could. If her parenting skills were in doubt, Connor's were even more so.

A strong surge of maternal yearning took her by surprise. She swallowed. She would not lose Dylan to the block of rock who stood in front of her.

The baby was hers.

Hers.

And she would fight with everything she possessed, every weapon at her disposal, to make sure Dylan stayed with her. She, at least, was capable of giving him love.

"He's not leaving here." She realized her voice had risen.

"Victoria, be sensible—"

"I'm being perfectly sensible."

He gave a snort. "With the hours you work you don't have time for a baby. Suzy told me—me and Michael," he amended as her brows drew together. "She was worried about you. She thought you'd buried yourself alive. All you lived for was building a practice that would lead to more status."

"Buried myself alive?" The idea that Suzy had discussed her with Connor hurt. "What about you? You started a new company—and not just any company, the Phoenix Corporation is a huge venture."

"Yes, but I employ a large staff, I delegate—I don't do everything myself. I still found time to visit Michael and Suzy—"

"You pig!" Victoria couldn't believe she'd heard right. "How can you say that? You cruel—"

"Oh, God, I'm sorry, Victoria." His chair crashed backward and he came toward her, his hands outstretched. "I didn't mean it that—"

She slapped his hands away. "You meant it exactly that way." Her fingers stung. She stared down at her reddening palms. The tears she'd stanched so fiercely for the past two days leaked out.

"Victoria, I'm sorry." His arms closed around her.

She fought him off, elbowing him fiercely. "Let go of me, damn you!"

He dropped his arms and stepped back, breathing heavily.

She stormed past him through the glass sliders. Half a dozen strides carried her across the living room and she yanked the front door open, her clammy hands clutching the door handle to keep her trembling knees from giving out. She'd wanted him to hold her, to share the grief…but never like this. "Get out."

"We need to talk about Dy—"

"I have nothing to say to you. Go."

"Victoria—"

She kept her gaze averted, horribly conscious of the soundless tears streaming down her face and the nausea rising in the back of her throat. "Please, just go."

He stumbled past her. At the last moment he turned. "If you need—"

Hot, blinding anger surged, and she said, "I don't need anything you can give me."

Without another word Connor left.

The funeral was finally over. Mourners huddled in groups in the church hall sipping coffee from white cups.

Connor glanced to where Victoria stood in silence beside three women who he assumed must've been friends of Suzy's. The scooped neckline of the fitted black dress she wore accentuated her collar bones and the delicate line of her throat, and her tall, slender body moved to-and-fro as she rocked

Dylan. But she didn't spare him a glance. She'd barely spoken to him today.

Guilt gnawed at him. How had he managed to screw up so royally two nights ago? Judging by the dark rings around her eyes, she hadn't slept since. She was hurting. He could feel it. Hell, she'd made him so mad, but that was no excuse. Nor did the knowledge that he'd never intended to wound her so deeply ease his guilt.

He was worse than the pig she'd called him.

She'd loved Suzy. She would never forgive him for implying that she'd neglected Suzy before her tragic death. And how could he blame her?

The baby's head was nestled close against her shoulder, and Dylan's eyes widened with interest as Connor came closer.

"Here, let me take the baby."

He saw her stiffen, her hold tighten around the baby, as she became aware of him. "No!"

Did she think he was going to rip the baby away from her?

"Please?" Couldn't she see his remorse? "Dylan must be heavy."

She edged away from the group she'd been standing with, but not before one of them gave him a strange look. He didn't care. It was Victoria that concerned him right now.

"We're fine."

Her pallor, her reddened eyes, the way her fingers dug into the blanket that swaddled Dylan gave lie to that. She so wasn't fine. But he wasn't about to argue with her here for everyone to see.

"Victoria…" Connor searched for the words that would mend everything between them, that would put them back into the state of almost-truce that had existed before his insensitive accusation. And came up dry.

"Go away," she hissed. "You're *not* taking the baby from me."

"Victoria—" An elegant woman with short hair wearing a black-and-white houndstooth suit came up beside them eyeing Connor with curiosity. "I wanted to say how sorry I am for the loss of your friend."

"Thank you, Bridget."

"And who is this fellow?" Bridget studied Dylan with decidedly wary eyes, causing Connor to suppress his first grin in days.

"This is Dylan, Suzy's baby."

"Oh." Bridget exchanged long looks with Victoria. "How dreadful. Is her family looking after him?"

"Suzy doesn't have any close family—her parents are dead, and she was an only child. Dylan's been staying with me."

His smile fading, Connor watched Bridget—whoever the hell she was—process that information silently. Victoria must have seen her doubts, too, because her arms tightened around the baby, causing Dylan to squawk in protest.

Connor reached for the wriggling baby. "I'll hold him for you." Dylan lurched toward him with a gurgle before Victoria could argue.

Bridget examined him with interest.

Connor nodded politely.

With visible reluctance Victoria performed the introductions. "Bridget, this is Connor North, a friend of the Masons. Connor, Bridget Edge is managing partner at Archer, Cameron and Edge."

"Connor North? Of the Phoenix Corporation?" Bridget's gaze sharpened. Connor could see her mentally tallying up his assets. "I didn't know you were connected to Phoenix, Victoria."

Victoria looked trapped.

Connor couldn't resist saying wickedly, "We've been friends for years. We met at Suzy and Michael's wedding—I was best man and Victoria was maid of honor."

"How romantic." Bridget gave him a thin smile before her

gaze settled back on Dylan. "This arrangement of looking after the baby isn't going to be permanent, is it?"

"No," said Connor.

"Yes," said Victoria, her color high.

Dylan blew a raspberry.

"Well, it sounds like you two have matters to sort out." Bridget's carefully plucked eyebrows were nearly up to her hairline. "Please call me at the office later, Victoria. I think we should talk."

The tension in Victoria's slim figure only increased with her boss's departure. As the last of the stragglers drifted out, leaving Connor alone with Victoria...and a sleeping Dylan in his car seat, he said, "Come, it's been a long day. Time for me to take the two of you home."

"You know I'm going to have to call the office," said Victoria.

Work. The funeral barely over and already she was fretting about work.

"All Frigid wants is for you to confirm that the baby won't interfere with your billable hours." Connor knew his cynicism was showing.

"Bridget. Her name is Bridget."

He kept his face deadpan. "I've always had a problem with names—you know that."

"Let it go, Connor." But her lips twitched.

So she did have a sense of humor. If he hadn't been watching her carefully he'd have missed that barely perceptible movement.

Outside the sky had turned gray and ominous, promising rain. As they headed toward the row of pines where the Maserati was parked, Connor said, "If Dylan comes to stay with me that will solve all her concerns."

"No."

So Victoria was digging in her heels. Connor knew the only way he was going to make her see sense was to be brutal.

"You'll never be able to raise a boy." Pausing beside the car, he set the infant seat down and opened the rear door. After securing the infant seat without waking Dylan, he turned back to Victoria and raked his gaze over her, telling her without words that he considered her wanting. "I give you two weeks tops before you surrender."

For a moment, he thought he'd shaken her. Then she narrowed her pinkened eyes. "You don't think I can do this? *I'm* the one who was watching him in the first place!"

Victoria had backbone, he had to give her that. But then, given her career he would've expected it. The question was: would she be able to cope all alone with a demanding job and a baby? He doubted it.

Connor took in her hands clenched in front of her breasts, and the way her mouth trembled. Her crushed-rose lips only emphasized her pallor. She looked too damned fragile.

For a moment he considered sweeping her into his arms, holding her close…

Then he shook the impulse away.

This was Victoria, not some frail butterfly. And she didn't need anything from him—she'd told him so herself.

He stepped closer to her. "That wasn't a dare. You don't need to prove anything to me. All I want is Dylan." And dammit, that was the truth of it. "Make it easy on yourself, let him stay with me." That's what he wanted desperately— what Michael would've wanted—his son to stay with him. But he couldn't say that. He'd already hurt her enough. "You can come and visit as often as you want."

The gold-green eyes that clashed with his were full of turbulence. "You think I haven't thought of letting him go to you? But I can't!"

"Why not?" he challenged.

"Because…" She gnawed at her lip.

"Because?" he prompted, forcing his gaze not to linger on her mouth.

"Don't ask this of me." There were shadows in her eyes that went way beyond grief. "I can't do it."

"It would be the easy solution."

She hesitated, clenching and unclenching her hands. "Easy solutions aren't always right. Suzy and I had been inseparable since we were five. I met her on our first day of school. Did you know that?"

He shook his head.

"She was tiny, like a beautiful, blue-eyed doll. She had blond curls, whereas I had dead straight, mousy hair. I felt so thin and tall next to her—she made me want to look after her."

Victoria's eyes had glazed over, and Connor knew she'd forgotten about him, about where they were, about the approaching storm. She was in a place he could not reach.

"We seemed like such opposites. Suzy so social, me so quiet."

"You were fortunate that your friendship endured for all those years."

"She was so much more than a friend. More than a sister, even. She was my confidante. My family. The person I trusted more than anyone else in the world when my family let me down." Her gaze cleared. "I can't give Dylan up. Don't ask it of me."

Connor's sigh went all the way to his soul. He'd already hurt her beyond belief with his swipe that she hadn't had time for Suzy before she died. How could he take her last link with her friend away from her? Even though he knew that Michael would've wanted Dylan to be with him.

The provision for sharing of guardianship and custody in the will had startled him. Victoria was a working woman who clearly didn't have time for bringing up a child. What had the Masons been thinking? Suzy must've insisted on it, never believing the will would have to be acted on long before Dylan grew to adulthood.

But whatever the will provided for, it was absolutely irrefutable that Suzy's death had left a vast chasm in Victoria's life.

Connor drew a deep breath and made the biggest concession of his life. Despite what he believed was the right thing for Dylan—and him, he would go along with the provisions of the will. "Then we'll have to split the custody—work out which of us gets which days."

Emotion flashed in her eyes. "How can you even suggest that? It took Dylan almost the whole weekend to settle with me. He's missing his parents, and now you're suggesting ripping him away from me."

"Not ripping," said Connor firmly. "We'll share him."

"And he's going to know what's happening?" She shook her head so hard the silken mass of her hair whipped from side to side. "No, he's not going to understand the terms of a custody arrangement. His parents are gone. Right now everything in his little life is in upheaval. I'm his only constant. How can you yank up the few roots he has left and take him away from me?"

She had a point. He remembered how Dylan had snuggled against her earlier.

"And you can't take Dylan away from my home. That's all that's familiar to him right now. Another change of place is going to unsettle him all over again."

He tilted his head to one side and replayed her words through his mind—*Another change of place is going to unsettle him all over again.* "That's it!"

At his exclamation Victoria stared at him as though he'd taken leave of his senses.

He hit a hand against his forehead. "The answer is simple."

Five

"Come on." Connor held open the door.

Victoria hesitated only for a second. No way was she abandoning Dylan to Connor and the powerful Maserati.

She stepped past Connor, catching a whiff of lemon and male, and settled into the passenger seat. The acreage of leather was seductively plush, and before she could protest Connor had leaned across her and clicked the seat restraint into place, strapping her in.

She'd barely recovered from the jolt to her senses of having him so close when he joined her in the intimacy of the cockpit.

"Ready?"

Victoria nodded, unsure what she was letting herself in for.

The motor roared, and the rich, husky voice of Nina Simone poured from the surround-sound system, silencing even Dylan. Connor's hands slid over the steering wheel with such tactile pleasure that Victoria had to suppress a groan. A moment later he swung the vehicle out of the churchyard.

The journey passed in a flash. As Connor throttled back the surging engine, Victoria glimpsed through the side window a familiar oak with wide, spreading branches.

What were they doing outside Suzy and Michael's home?

She struggled impotently to unlock the car door, until—to her immense frustration—Connor strode around and freed her.

Clambering out, she slung her tote over her shoulder and asked, "Why have you brought us here, Connor?"

"Let me get Dylan first."

Nostalgia welled up as she stared at the Edwardian cottage that had been Suzy and Michael's home since their marriage—and where she had spent so many happy hours.

She wandered across the sidewalk to the low, white wooden gate.

Dylan had been baptized in this garden. Right there in the arbor tucked into the east side, under the canopy of girly, pale-pink roses. It had been one of the few times she and Connor had visited the house at the same time. As the baby's godparents they'd been forced to put on a façade of friendship for Michael and Suzy's sakes.

The gate swung open under her touch. As she stepped onto the winding garden path a gigantic wave of sadness drowned her. The ghosts of Suzy's laughter and Michael's slow smiles lurked everywhere. In the pretty pansies that brightened the pots lining the pathway, in the fresh coat of lily-white paint on the shutters and in the shriek of a gull overhead, its wings icy-pale against the darkening sky.

She started as Connor came up beside her.

"Connor, I'm not sure that I'm ready to do this. I don't think I can even go into the cottage yet." A tempest of grief was imminent. Only Connor's presence held the tears in check. "I need time."

"Look." Connor swung the baby seat forward. "I think Dylan knows he's home."

The baby was cricking his neck, and making gurgling sounds of pleasure.

Sorrow tasted bitter in the back of her mouth. What did poor Dylan know? "It's not his home anymore," she choked. "Michael and Suzy are gone."

And she and Connor were going to have to decide—and agree—what to do with the house.

Michael had done a marvelous job restoring the old cottage—with Suzy and Connor's help. But the maintenance would be a nightmare. Best to sell it and invest the proceeds for Dylan.

Moisture escaped from the corner of one eye and she quickly brushed it away before Connor could notice.

He swung around. "I've been thinking…"

She gave a surreptitious sniff. "What?"

"One of the reasons you felt that Dylan should live with you was because he's grown accustomed to his surroundings in the past few days."

"Well, yes…" It looked like she'd gotten through to him. Finally. The first thread of relief started to unwind. She glanced up at him, grateful for his understanding. "It'll be much better for him than going to your home, which he doesn't know."

"I wouldn't say he doesn't know it," Connor objected. "He has been there with his parents. But as you pointed out, it would be much better for him to be in familiar surroundings— like here."

"*Here?*" Dismay filled her.

Connor nodded. "This is, after all, his home."

In the distance thunder growled. Victoria decided that even the weather gods disagreed with Connor.

"Oh, no, I couldn't live here." The comforting sense of relief had vanished. There were far too many memories of Suzy and Michael. In every piece of painted wood, every flower. It would kill her to have to live here. "Don't ask me to do that."

"I'm not asking you to—I'll move in. Can't you see?" He was looking at her as if he expected her to applaud his perspicacity. "You were right, Victoria. And this way I won't be displacing the baby. He'll be in familiar surroundings."

Her own arguments had caused him to come to this conclusion? Her heart started to thud in fear. She was going to lose Dylan after all. "You can't do this!"

He thrust his hand into his pants pocket and brought out a bunch of keys. "Why not?"

Because Dylan is mine, she thought. But she couldn't tell him that. She'd promised Suzy she wouldn't reveal her part in Dylan's birth.

Oh, dear God.

She tried to get her thoughts straight. Surely Suzy's death released her from that promise.

Or did it?

She rubbed her fingertips against the sides of her nose. Finally she said thinly, "It's macabre that you're thinking of moving into their home when we only buried them today." Her head started to ache. "Tell me you don't mean this?"

But Connor was already striding up the path that wound to the wooden front door, keys jangling between his fingers, the handle of the infant seat hooked over his arm.

A splatter of moisture landed on her arm. Victoria glanced up, startled at how dark the sky had grown. She hurried after Connor and grabbed his arm.

He swung around. "Careful, you'll awaken—"

"I'm not going in there. I'm not." Barely conscious of the wetness on her cheeks, Victoria tipped her head back and glared at him defiantly.

Connor grew still. His free hand came up and touched her cheek with gentle fingers. "You're crying."

She ducked her head sideways, dislodging his touch. "I'm not crying. It's the rain." It seemed important to convince him of that. To reveal no weakness. Victoria pointed to the sky. "Look how low the clouds are."

But his gaze didn't waver from her face, and his eyes softened to the color of mist. "Okay, it's the rain."

"It's going to get worse." She wiped her eyes with the back of her hand. "We can't stay out here. Dylan will get drenched." Hunching her shoulders, she threw a haunted glance toward the cottage.

"I'll take the two of you home." Connor put an arm around her shoulder and turned her toward the gate, the infant seat swinging gently from his other hand.

The warmth of his body against hers flooded Victoria with a rush of emotion. She blinked frantically as he held the garden gate open for her, determined not to cry any more. This was Connor, why was he being so darned gentle? It made her want to cry all the more.

The rain began to fall in stinging drops. Connor dropped his arm from her shoulders and hurried to get Dylan into the back of the Maserati.

Victoria stood on the sidewalk, unmindful as the drops turned to sheets of water. She'd won. She could hardly believe it. He wasn't going to force her—or Dylan—to go into the cottage. Conner was taking them both home.

So why didn't she feel a thrill of victory? Why did she feel so terribly lost?

"You need to get out of that wet dress."

Connor jerked his gaze away from the sodden material that clung to Victoria's skin, blatantly revealing the gentle curves and the tight tips of her breasts as she shivered.

"But Dylan—"

"Is perfectly dry. I got him into the car before the heavens opened." Connor's attention fell onto the baby still sleeping in his infant seat.

"He's exhausted."

He knew without looking that she'd followed his gaze. Victoria must be exhausted, too. After all, she'd been holding the baby for most of the day. But if he said anything more, she'd only deny it. So Connor settled himself down onto a couch and propped his feet up on the coffee table. "Why don't you go have a hot shower. I'll watch the baby for a while."

Edging forward, she said, "Why don't you make yourself at home?"

"Not now, Victoria." Weariness crept into his voice. He'd had enough of all the sniping between them.

She stared at him for a long moment, then bowed her head. "I'm sorry."

Connor nodded and closed his eyes. Hearing so sound of movement, he cracked them open. She hadn't moved. She stood in front of him, looking every bit as drained as he felt.

"You'll feel better after a shower."

"Maybe." Her hazel eyes remained fixed on him. "But right not I don't really want to be alone."

"Oh, Victoria!"

Her reluctant admission moved him. She was so fiercely independent. Connor knew for her to reveal any weakness at all meant she must be feeling utterly empty. Dropping his legs down, he reached forward and scooped her off her feet. She landed across his lap with a squeak, a struggling mass of arms and legs.

"I'm wet!" she wailed. "I'm going to soak you, too."

"Shh." He bent his head over hers. "Just relax."

Her body softened instantly. For long minutes he held her, not speaking, not thinking, simply savoring the scent of her, the softness of her body under his soothing palm that rubbed along her back in long strokes.

At last she shifted. "I must be heavy."

Connor almost groaned as her bottom moved in his lap. Heat shot through his spine and he fought the urge to shudder in reaction. If she'd only stayed still…

Victoria froze. Her head came up, and startled golden-green eyes met his. Connor knew she'd felt his unmistakable reaction. He waited for her to pull away. She didn't.

"Victoria…?"

With a groan he pulled her toward him. Her parted lips met his, and he sucked in the whisper of her breath. It was a hungry kiss, full of pent-up emotion, of passion long resisted. Connor licked the soft sweetness of her bottom lip, tasting her deeply, and she wriggled closer.

His fingers found the zipper of her dress, and he broke off the kiss. The rasp of the sliding zipper cut across the sound of their ragged breathing. Connor peeled the wet fabric off her shoulders and slid the dress over her hips, down her legs, his gaze all the time holding hers, watching as a flush of passion flooded her pale cheeks.

When the dress was off, he pulled her atop him so that her bare legs straddled his hips. Her naked skin shimmered in the evening light, as pale as pearl against the seductive black satin bra and panties. Connor's breath caught at the sheer grace of her long limbs and sweet curves.

With shaking fingers she reached forward and undid the buttons of his shirt. "Your shirt is damp, too."

"Just a little." He'd gotten wet holding the car door open for her.

Pulling the edges apart, she murmured, "Then it will also have to come off."

Connor leaned forward and shrugged his arms out of the sleeves. "Anything you say."

A glint lit her eyes, and her lips curved into a delicious smile. "You should always be so amenable."

"I'm at your mercy." He stared at her rosy lush mouth.

She laughed. Driven by an impulse he could not resist, Connor reached out a shaky finger and outlined the full, wide, laughing curse. Her mirth died away, and the pink tip of her tongue came out and touched his finger.

"You undo me, woman," he said hoarsely, "with one little flick of your tongue."

"Then what about this?" She trailed a tantalizing finger down his chest, across his stomach, before halting an inch above his belt.

"Tease," he groaned.

"Your skin is so silken," whispered Victoria.

His erection leapt. "That's my line," he growled, yanking her to him and bending his head forward to ravenously plant a row of kisses along the tempting arch of her throat. Under his lips he felt her throat contract as she gasped. His mouth opened, and he tongued the silky skin. His open mouth slid down, over the narrow slip of black satin that joined the cups of her bra covering her breasts…down farther…savoring the sweetness of her flesh.

Grasping her hips between his hands, he lifted her up and kissed the smooth skin of her belly.

"Connor!" The sound was guttural, full of need and desire.

"Be patient." His erection strained again his pants, rigid with desperation. He wasn't so sure that he was capable of following his own command.

She pulled away and settled back astride his lap.

Connor's back arched instinctively at the contact. "My God, woman."

He felt the buckle of his belt give under the persuasion of her nimble fingers. His heart skipped a beat as she undid the button below. The sound of his breathing filled the room, hoarse and jagged.

Light danced across his eyelids as he squeezed his eyes shut. Sliding his hands up her sleek back, he reached the catch of her bra and fumbled, his fingers suddenly clumsy.

A cry filled the air.

Victoria's hands stilled. "Dylan."

She scrambled off his lap, tugging the clinging black dress over her breasts, and ran to the other side of the room. Lifting the baby out of the infant seat, she turned her head, and Connor's throat closed up as he read the turbulent confusion in her eyes.

Bewilderment. Guilt. Shame.

And, underneath it all, the heat of desire, too.

Connor rose slowly to his feet.

"Put your shirt back on." Her voice was a thready croak.

"It's damp."

"Please," she implored.

"Okay." He pulled it on and watched as she tried to juggle the baby while trying to push her arms back into the wet sleeves of her dress. "Give Dylan here—I'll entertain him while you change."

Without meeting his gaze, she thrust the baby into his arms and fled.

How could he have allowed—no, encouraged—that to happen?

Victoria couldn't believe that she'd almost ended up having sex with Connor. She fastened her jeans and reached for a lambs wool sweater. If Dylan hadn't woken up…

Oh, God!

How could she have been so foolish? And now she had to leave her bedroom to go back downstairs. She groaned in dismay. It would take all her courage to face Connor after what had happened. And to demand that he never touch her again. They both had a duty to Dylan. As his guardians. Passion couldn't be allowed to interfere with their responsibilities.

As Dylan's mother, she couldn't afford to risk alienating

she raised her head—and clashed with Connor's intense gaze. Her stomach rolled over.

Victoria drew a steadying breath. Now was not the time to be sucked in by Connor's lethal charisma. She wasn't looking for a man. And he was the last one on earth that she'd pick. Surely she hadn't forgotten that?

He was all wrong for her—he'd just proved it beyond a shadow of a doubt. He'd never let her retain the financial and emotional independence she'd fought so hard to attain. He'd want a woman who he could control and command. A woman who would give up work at his demand. And that would never be her.

She would never risk being at the mercy of a man's whims. As her mother had been. It wasn't only the woman who suffered, but her children too. She had first-hand experience of what happened when children paid the price of impulsive passion.

But she wasn't about to lose custody of the only son she'd have. So Victoria said carefully, "Yes. And I'm going to take a leaf out of your book and delegate more—hire a junior for me. That's just one more thing I need to discuss with

Connor. It would be the height of irresponsibility to let passion rule her—and make her no better than her parents had been.

By the time she entered the living room, she'd pulled herself together, making sure that none of her trepidation showed. The man who'd kissed her to distraction was sitting on the carpet, and the contents of the baby's diaper bag were strewn around the room.

Connor looked up at her entrance and gave her a sheepish grin. "I figured out how to change his diaper."

Victoria yanked her gaze away from the chest she'd run her fingers over. Thankfully he'd covered the glorious muscles up with a shirt as she'd requested.

"Congratulations," she managed and searched for the words to tell him that she did not want him to ever kiss her again—that it was a dereliction of their duties as Dylan's guardians.

Dylan chose that moment to flap his arms and, gazing at her accusingly, he started to cry. Victoria picked him up, taking care not to brush against Connor's legs.

"He's hungry." Forcing herself to glance at Connor, she said, "There's a bottle ready in the fridge. Won't you fetch it please?"

To Victoria's surprise, Connor went without demur.

As the minutes passed, Dylan grew increasingly fractious. Victoria jiggled him up and down, hushing him, but to no avail, so she started to sing.

When Connor came back, Dylan's cries intensified at the sight of the bottle.

"Give me a second, Dyl." As Dylan protested she removed the plastic seal and replaced the top of the bottle, then sank onto the plump cushions of the couch and positioned him in the crook of her arm. "There you go," she murmured, giving him the bottle.

She resumed humming a snatch of "Big Rock Candy Mountain," then ceased as she became aware of Connor watching her, a smile lurking around his mouth.

"Don't stop."

Flushing, and terribly self-conscious under his intense scrutiny, she said, "I don't hum—or sing—very well."

"It sounded fine to me, and more importantly Dylan liked it. Look, he's complaining because you've stopped."

Victoria glanced down to see Dylan's mouth working frantically, his tongue clearly visible as he prepared to let out a loud bellow.

"That's not my humming he's missing—it's the teat." Victoria offered the dislodged teat to him and the baby latched on with gusto.

She slanted a faint smile up at Connor. "But thanks for saying he was missing it, even if it was the tallest tale I've ever heard."

"It wasn't that bad."

"It was worse, but we'll keep that our secret, okay?"

He gave her a long look. "Our secret."

Suddenly feeling as if her skin had grown too tight, Victoria pulled Dylan closer. The silence surrounding the three of them seemed to quiver.

What in heaven's name was happening to her? Victoria started to hum again. Anything to break that seething quiet. After a while she switched over to "Old MacDonald Had a Farm" and Connor joined in.

Dylan sucked the last dregs out of the bottle and his eyelids started to droop.

"I've been thinking…"

Instantly Connor had all her attention. "What?"

"Dylan should stay here."

Euphoria swept Victoria along. She'd gotten what she'd wanted. Now she had to make it work, prove to Connor it was the right thing for Dylan. "I'm so glad you realized I was right."

His gaze narrowed to cool slits and all the easygoing camaraderie evaporated. "Hang on, we're not changing the custody

arrangement of the will. He stays with you for now, but we'll review the arrangement in a month."

No, that wasn't what she'd intended.

She considered arguing that his solution only meant unsettling Dylan later down the line, then decided to quit while she was still ahead. When the time came, she was sure she be able to convince him that Dylan would be better off st ing with her. As for her resolve to tell Connor that she w to keep their relationship formal as Dylan's guardi appeared that would not be necessary. Connor was ness. He certainly showed no signs of being a m whelmed by desire. She suppressed a ridiculo something suspiciously like disappointment.

He was speaking again. "Dylan needs you. it—you're so good with him."

Victoria stared at him, astonished. Conno was good with Dylan? He wasn't the kind of n praise. A surge of happiness swept her. So fears that she'd be terrible at the motherin

He was still talking. "But it's going career track."

"I know, and I've come to terms with to speak to Bridget and tell her that sh late into the evenings anymore. Sh smile that faded a little as his gaze made her shiver inside.

"So you'll need to take leave

Take leave? Averting her fa bottle on the coffee table. H cially now when everyone capacity. She'd tell him taking leave. Now was n his decision to leave Dyl

When she was sure she hac

Six

After Connor had gone, Victoria called Bridget Edge.

The assurance that Victoria would be at work the following day was met with a sigh of undisguised relief. And after a small pause Bridget had agreed to Victoria's suggestion that hiring a junior accountant would be a good idea—provided, of course, that Victoria's client base kept growing.

Victoria set the phone down and closed her eyes. For the first time since learning of Michael and Suzy's deaths her sense of optimism blossomed again.

Everything was going to work out.

She quashed the growing apprehension that Connor would not be happy with the outcome.

The next day, Victoria dropped Dylan at the day care center that Suzy had enrolled Dylan in. Leaving him was a terrible wrench, but she assuaged her guilt by slipping out during lunch time to check on him. One of the young day care employees murmured that the baby hadn't settled and appeared to be fretting.

Of course Dylan was fretting.

Poor baby! Victoria picked him up, inhaling the scent of powder and baby. Dylan was missing Suzy and Michael. And she'd left him in this unfamiliar place. Guilt overwhelmed her. She'd added to his sense of dislocation—but what other choice did she have?

Connor, a little voice said, she could have called Connor for help. He'd offered to take the baby. But if she called him he would crow in victory—and claim Dylan.

She would lose her baby.

And Connor wouldn't look after the baby personally, either. He'd simply hire a nanny, which was no different from what she was doing. Dylan wriggled in her arms. Victoria kissed his head apologetically and loosened her grip.

But what if she confided in Connor that she was Dylan's biological mother? Would he understand…would he be prepared to compromise? She nuzzled Dylan's soft baby hair and thought of the Connor North she knew….

Hard. Decisive. Ruthless. There wasn't a compromising bone in that strong, too-male body.

No. She couldn't tell him.

She would have to get through this by herself.

The rest of the day passed in a rush. And Victoria, who'd intended to leave not long after lunch for the first time in her life, left work far later than she'd intended.

Dylan still hadn't settled by the Victoria went to collect him. But the staff were sure Monday would be better.

The weekend went by in a blur of sleepless exhaustion. Victoria missed a call from Connor while she and Dylan napped, and after listening to the recording of his deep, provocative voice saying, "Just wanted to see if you're coping," decided against phoning him back.

So he thought she wasn't coping?

Well, she certainly wasn't going to cry for help.

By the following Tuesday Dylan was visibly querulous, and one of the day care workers called to say he was running a slight temperature.

Panic flooded Victoria and she wasted no time getting to the day care center.

"He didn't drink his last bottle." The day care attendant looked concerned. "If his temperature rises further you may want to take him to the doctor."

By the time Victoria got Dylan home, after an hour in peak-hour traffic, he was hot and flushed. Pausing only to take his temperature, which had rocketed alarmingly, she faced the fact that this was more than grief and dislocation. Dylan was ill.

A call to her doctor garnered his pager. Victoria swore. But within minutes a doctor on call had phoned and told her to take the baby to the nearest medical center. Berating herself for leaving it so long, she hoisted Dylan into the baby seat, secured him and hurried to the front door.

Connor had been waiting all week for Victoria to phone and beg him to take Dylan, to admit defeat. But she hadn't. To his annoyance she hadn't even responded to the message he'd left on her answering service. And Connor was left wishing he'd never allowed the hollowness in her eyes to persuade him to leave Dylan in her care. What had he been thinking? Dylan was the most important person in his life.

Five days had passed since the funeral, and he couldn't wait any longer. The driving urge to see Dylan—a primal, deeply-rooted need to reassure himself that his baby was happy—dominated him. Yet as the Maserati ate up the now-familiar route Connor admitted it wasn't only Dylan he'd been missing—he wanted to see Victoria, too.

It was perfectly normal, this desire to spend time with her.

Right. It was perfectly normal to crave the presence of someone who drove you crazy?

Connor's mouth slanted.

They'd each lost someone they loved—an aching loss that the other understood better than anyone else in existence. That made sense. But it wasn't convincing. It sure didn't explain why the shape of her wide mouth haunted him when he should've been thinking about work. Or why the memory of her slender body bending over Dylan's car seat could wake him in the middle of the night, even though he'd always preferred blondes with hourglass curves. Or why he kept fantasizing about the silken softness of her skin under his fingertips.

Hell, he'd even wondered how she'd coped with telling Bridget she was taking more time off work to look after the baby. He'd actually considered calling earlier in the week to see if she needed support.

But he'd managed to hold out.

Until now.

As he lifted his hand to ring her doorbell the front door flew open.

"Oh, you startled me."

His first thought was that he must have been blind. Victoria was beautiful. How had he ever missed it? How had he ever thought her plain?

Her long hair swirled about a face that was simply perfect. Straight, uncompromising brows, direct hazel eyes and a wide mouth of such delicious rosy-red that he fought the urge to kiss it.

Then he saw that she was upset.

His gaze dropped to the infant seat. "Are you going out?"

"Dylan isn't well. I'm taking him to the medical center."

Connor didn't ask questions. "We'll go in my car."

When she looked like she wanted to protest, he added, "If I drive you can look after Dylan."

She nodded.

Once he'd made sure she and Dylan were comfortably ensconced in the back seat of the Maserati, Connor pulled out his cell phone and made a call, before climbing into the driver's seat.

"This isn't the medical center I meant," Victoria said sharply fifteen minutes later.

Connor felt the impact of her accusing gaze on the back of his head, but he didn't shift his eyes from the road ahead. "I called a friend who's a pediatrician. He's meeting us at his rooms—he understands the background."

Chuck had known Michael, and knew Connor had been named guardian of his child. Chuck even knew the truth about Dylan's paternity. "If it's necessary Chuck will admit Dylan to Starship," he said, referring to the well-known children's hospital.

"Chuck?" She sounded doubtful. "How do you know him?"

"His name is Charles Drysdale, if that's any better. We play squash at the same club." A stab of pain pierced Connor at the thought of visiting the courts without Michael. "And he's one of the best pediatricians in town. You'll be charmed—most women are."

Charles—or Chuck—Drysdale had twinkling eyes and a way of putting patients at ease within minutes of meeting him. Victoria liked him at once.

"Tell me what you noticed, Victoria," he asked when she'd taken Dylan out of the infant seat and sat down with him on her lap.

Victoria shifted guiltily in the chair, all too conscious of Connor hovering anxiously behind her. "Dylan has been a little crabby for a couple of days."

Connor came closer and scowled. "You never let me know."

"I thought he was missing his parents," she said defensively.

"He'd certainly notice that," Chuck said. "So two days? That's how long he's been crabby?"

Victoria thought back to how demanding the baby had been over the weekend, how only holding him had settled him. "Maybe a little longer—from Friday perhaps. The funeral was on Thursday and he seemed fine then. But I can't say for sure."

Chuck made a note on the pad in front of him. "Did you notice anything else?"

"Li called me at work earlier. Dylan had a temperature and—"

"Who is Li?" Connor paced closer.

Victoria shrank into the chair. "She's one of the caregivers in the day care center."

"Day care center? What's Dylan doing in a day care center?" Connor's eyes glittered with the kind of rage she'd never seen. "We've *never* discussed putting Dylan in a day care center."

Chuck held up a hand. "Connor, save it for later. Let's see what's wrong with the baby first." The doctor rose to his feet and crossed the room to an examining couch. He gave Victoria a sympathetic smile. "Why don't you bring Dylan here?"

Victoria felt totally wretched as she laid Dylan down on the bed. Every doubt she'd ever had about mothering crashed in on her. "I'm not doing a good job, am I?"

"You're doing just fine. Most new mothers feel a little frazzled and uncertain when their baby becomes ill."

He asked some more questions while he examined Dylan. Finally he said, "Have you ever had chicken pox, Victoria?"

"Chicken pox? That's what Dylan has?"

"Certainly looks like it. It's not common for such young babies to get chicken pox, but it does happen, and the symptoms fit—the temperature, not drinking…and see here?"

She stared down to where he pointed to a small pink dot on Dylan's chest. "And here." He indicated another spot, this one with a small scab.

"I saw that—I thought it was an insect bite. But shouldn't there be more spots?"

"Not necessarily. Some cases only have a few spots here and there."

Lifting her head, she said, "But I thought chicken pox spots were watery blisters."

"That one," he gestured to the pink dot, "will blister soon. Then it will scab over."

Victoria stared at Chuck, conscious of an overwhelming sense of relief. Dylan wasn't going to die. It wasn't scarlet fever or convulsions or some incurable disease. "He'll be all right, won't he?"

"Plenty of fluids, calamine lotion and cool baths. I'll prescribe some acetaminophen for Dylan and a mild sedative for you. Is there anyone to help you with the baby? He'll need to stay home for a week. And you need some rest."

Oh, no. She gave a groan. "I need to go to work."

"I'll give you a note."

What would Bridget and the rest of the partners say? "I can't, I've taken too much time off already."

"Your body needs rest if you've been up the kind of hours I suspect this young man has been keeping." Chuck drew a card from a holder on the nearby table. "This is for a nursing service. They'll be able to assist you over the next week, although he can go back to the day care center once he's better."

"That must be where he picked this up," Connor growled from behind her.

Victoria felt awful, and remorse set in afresh.

"He could've come into contact with the virus anywhere." Chuck shrugged. "But the incubation period is ten to twenty days, so given the time he's been at the day care center it's highly unlikely he contracted chicken pox there."

Victoria could've kissed Chuck. *It wasn't her fault.* But the feeling of relief that numbed her knees turned to horror as she heard Chuck ask Connor, "Have you had chicken pox?"

Connor nodded.

"Good, then you can help Victoria."

Connor's angry gaze bored into her. "Don't worry, I intend to."

Misery sank like a dark cloud over Victoria. He would take Dylan away from her. She really didn't need the only kind of help Connor was prepared to give.

"Thanks so much for taking us to Charles Drysdale. He's such a nice doctor."

Connor listened to Victoria's polite babble as she whipped the sleeping Dylan through the front door, set the infant seat down on the white carpet and swung the door closed in Connor's face.

Before it could click shut he threw his full weight forward against the wood. "Not so fast," he growled, sticking a foot in the crack.

Folding her arms, she blocked the gap he'd leveraged open. "If you don't mind I need to see to the baby."

"I mind very much," he said with slow menace that caused her hazel eyes to turn gold in startled fear.

"It's late, Connor. Can't this wait until tomorrow?"

"No!" He'd done with compromise. Now they would do things his way.

He shouldered the door open. She shrank back. Damn right she should be scared. Right now he was too furious to pay much attention to her fears.

"What are you going to do tomorrow? Take more leave?"

"I can't—I'm in the middle of…" Her voice trailed away

as his frown deepened. Then she drew a deep breath and ran her fingers through her hair. "To be honest, I haven't had a chance to think what I'm going to do. Perhaps I'll hire a nurse."

"And leave the baby with someone you've never met?" The anger that had been smoldering since he'd first discovered she'd lied to him about taking leave and had taken Dylan to a center full of other babies reignited.

"I'll make sure I get someone with good references."

"You won't need to."

Fear shadowed the gold-green eyes. "What do you mean?"

"We agreed that you would take leave!"

"*You* demanded that I take leave—I never agreed."

Connor ran his hands through his hair and tried to remember back to what had been said. "Well, you certainly never objected. You know I'd assumed you'd agreed."

"Did I?" But her gaze flickered away.

"You lied to me by omission, Victoria." He bore down on her. "How dare you take the baby to day care without consulting me? We hold joint custody, remember...or are you trying to get me angry enough to apply to court to have that revoked?"

She looked shaken. "You can't do that."

"I can—and I will if you persist in this stupidity. What's important here is Dylan's well-being."

"Everything I've done has been in Dylan's interests."

"No, it isn't." His rage boiled over. "You're only looking after your interests—your damned career that's so important to you. Not caring for a grieving baby!" He shook his head. "God, but you make me sick!"

She went white. "I—"

He couldn't let that air of deceptive feminine fragility sway him. "Spare me from ambitious women who walk over everyone to get what they want."

A sprinkling of freckles he'd never noticed before stood

out in sharp relief against her pallor. "I would never jeopardize Dylan for my career—"

"Never?" he said softly. "That's why you took a young baby to a nursery full of other children where he could pick up viruses?"

"Chuck said—"

"That it was unlikely, not that it was impossible." He leaned closer until his nose was up against hers. "Do you think that's what Suzy wanted for her baby?"

She stumbled back. "Suzy enrolled Dylan in that center. I've done nothing Suzy would not have done herself."

That caused him to hesitate, but only for an instant. Dylan was his son. When he thought what might have happened… Damn, he'd never be able to trust her with Dylan again. "Why the hell didn't you call me?" he snarled.

She remained mute.

Of everything, it was the not calling that enraged him most. She was so pigheaded, so stubborn she would've let the baby come to harm before she called him.

His baby.

What had once been a favor to a devastated friend, a random donation of sperm, had turned into the most important thing in his life. Dylan was more precious than anything in the world. And she hadn't bothered to tell him that his baby was sick. The baby he'd entrusted her with against his own better judgment.

A surge of sheer instinctive paternal possessiveness shook him as he stalked closer. "It was an unforgivable mistake not to call me."

Pinned against the wall, she faced him. The glaze of shock had receded and her eyes shot sparks at him. "You would've taken Dylan away from me."

"Oh, for…" He broke off before the force of the crude curse erupted.

She squeezed her eyes shut.

Recognizing how real her dread was, Connor stepped back and leashed the anger that vibrated through his large frame. "This has gone far enough. I'm taking the baby with me."

"No." There was raw pain in the sound. "You can't!"

"You'll find that I can."

Victoria's head came up. Her cheeks were stained with hectic color, a vivid contrast to her previous bleached paleness. "No. Michael and Suzy wanted us to share custody. I can only see one way that this can work."

"What's that?"

"I'm coming to live with you, too."

Connor gave her an incredulous stare. The silence reverberated with tension. Then he said, "Fine. You can come, too!"

Seven

Victoria walked into Connor's palatial home for the first time the next evening, not sure of what she would find.

What she didn't expect was to see Connor lying on his back on the thick carpet in the living room, bouncing above him a bathed, ecstatic Dylan. She hesitated in the doorway and watched as Dylan squealed in delight and Connor whooped.

A long-forgotten sense of being the outsider swept her, of being the kid with the mother who slept all day while her father blew in and out of town like tumbleweed.

Then Connor caught sight of her, and flashed her a dizzying smile. "Look, Dylan, there's Victoria."

She dropped her leather laptop case and took a step forward. Dylan stretched his arms toward her. She swung him up and buried her nose against his neck. He smelled clean, of baby powder and calamine lotion. He made soft snuffling sounds and her heart melted.

"How was your day?" Connor had sat up, the laughter fading from his face as his eyes became watchful.

She let out a deep breath. "A lot better than yesterday." Knowing that Dylan was being looked after by Connor's housekeeper had lifted a great weight off her shoulders.

"How's Dylan been?" She set the baby down on the floor and, dropping down beside him, she tugged his T-shirt up.

"Ratty a little earlier. But he had a good sleep."

"The spots are looking better, not so red."

"He was fussing so I bathed him…and the cool water seemed to settle him."

"He loves his bath." Victoria searched Connor's chest for signs that Dylan had splashed with his usual abandon but he looked as immaculate as ever. Typical. If it had been her, her shirt would be clinging to her.

"I think you can handle bath time from now on. You must do a far better job."

His grin flashed back. "I've changed—both my jeans and shirt looked like candidates for the wettest wet."

"Oh." Victoria instantly felt better. "I've arranged for some of my things to be delivered tomorrow. I'll put the rest into storage and let the town house."

"I've made some calls," Connor said. "I'll be interviewing for an au pair for Dylan tomorrow during the morning."

"But I thought we'd do that together." He was doing it again—taking over, marginalizing her involvement. And underlining her own insecurities. "I want to have input into the person that we hire."

Connor frowned. "I've already arranged the interviews, and I'll be working from home until I employ an au pair. It's not fair to leave Moni with the house and Dylan."

"Moni?"

"My housekeeper. I'll introduce you shortly."

"Thanks," she said brusquely. "But I'd appreciate it if you would rearrange the interviews for when I come home. We've got joint guardianship—and that means we're partners, we consult each other and make joint decisions." That would be hard for him. Connor North didn't have a compromising bone in that powerful, autocratic body.

Her gaze dwelled for a moment on the strong shoulders, the determined jaw, then locked with his unreadable gray gaze. A shivery awareness caused her to shift her attention back to the baby wriggling on the carpet.

"I want to satisfy myself that the person looking after Dylan is the best candidate we can get."

"And you don't trust me to find that person?"

She thought of his track record. He hadn't done a great job picking trustworthy people to surround himself with in the past. Dana Fisher and Paul Harper had turned out to be faithless. But she couldn't very well remind him of that.

Instead she said stubbornly, "I'm coguardian, I have a right to be involved."

"You're determined to make this as difficult as possible, aren't you?"

Victoria shook her head. "I just want to make sure you choose the right person."

So the next day, in consultation with Victoria, Connor rescheduled the interviews. Two were set for that night and one for Friday evening. The first candidate, a young woman with impeccable qualifications, had already arrived by the time Victoria came home from work, late and flustered.

After ten minutes' easy conversation with Anne Greenside, Connor had decided she was the perfect choice.

But Victoria clearly had other ideas. "I see most of your jobs have involved older children," she quizzed Anne.

"I love babies," Anne said with a sincerity Connor found convincing.

"But you can't stay late?"

Connor had known that would be a stumbling block the moment he'd seen the woman's resume. Despite her devotion to Dylan, Victoria was ambitious. Work would always come first. She would want a nanny who could work late. On a regular basis. He didn't have to cast his mind back far to remember the kind of hours Dana had worked.

"I live with my invalid mother—she needs me at night. But I can start tomorrow, if that makes it easier for you and your husband."

"We're not married—Dylan's not even our baby," Victoria blurted out.

"I'm sorry. I wasn't aware of that." But Anne looked curiously from one to the other.

"My fault," said Connor easily, "I should've explained the situation to the agency." He quickly filled her in.

"Poor baby." Anne looked stricken. "He's fortunate to have the two of you. But it's not going to be easy for him as he grows up."

"What do you mean?" Victoria asked first.

"He'll always have questions—he's not like other children now. His parents' death has seen to that."

"He'll have us."

Connor could feel Victoria's growing tension.

"Yes, but you're not his parents. You aren't planning to adopt him—" She looked at them enquiringly.

Connor shook his head slowly.

"We haven't discussed it," Victoria said repressively.

After Anne had left, Connor said. "I like her. She's perfect. We should offer her the position before someone else snaps her up."

Victoria shook her head. "I don't agree. And she's very opinionated."

But Anne had said spoken the truth. It was in Dylan's interests for them to consider all points of view. But Connor bit his tongue. He should've expected this. When had Victoria ever agreed with him? Yet, instead of accusing her of merely trying to frustrate him, he drew a deep breath. "Her references are fantastic."

"I still need to call and verify them. I can only do that tomorrow." She glanced at him. "Anyway, we have to see the others. I'd like you to keep an open mind while we interview them."

Before he could respond the next candidate had arrived. It didn't take long for Connor to catch Victoria's eye. She looked equally dubious.

He relaxed a little. His concerns that Victoria might oppose him simply for the hell of it evaporated.

They thanked the woman for coming and Connor saw her out.

When he returned to the study Victoria said, "She was awful."

"Agreed." That must be a first. He started to grin and Victoria smiled back, her mouth wide and luscious. Instantly, heat spread through him.

"I want someone older. Steadier."

Connor forced his gaze away from her mouth and tried to focus on what she was saying. "Not too old."

Victoria stuck her bottom lip out in that infuriating way that he'd come to recognize meant trouble.

"I can see you've already decided on Anne," she said. "You should've waited until I came before you started the interview."

The warmth and desire that had filled him evaporated. "Don't be unreasonable. I didn't start it alone by design. You were late."

"Something came up." But she looked abashed. "It won't happen tomorrow."

* * *

But when Victoria rushed home on Friday evening, it was to find that the third prospect had cancelled. And Connor had gone ahead and employed Anne.

"I called. You were in a meeting," he said to her intense fury.

"You should've waited."

"I didn't want to mess around and lose Anne," he said with patient logic that infuriated her further.

After giving Dylan his bottle that night, Victoria headed downstairs in her nightgown and dressing gown to make herself a cup of tea in the state-of-the-art kitchen, still annoyed at his take-charge actions.

She drank the hot tea, and thought how lovely it had been to come home to a hot meal that Connor's housekeeper had prepared. Usually she was too tired at night to make much more than a sandwich for dinner.

When she'd finished her tea and rinsed out the cup, she felt much better, and wearily wound her way up the stairs to her room—suite of rooms, she amended. A large bathroom and two bedrooms led off the sitting room. The smaller of the bedrooms had been converted into a nursery—complete with pale-blue walls and bright-yellow ducks stenciled as a border.

She pushed open the nursery door. As her eyes adjusted to the dimness from the night-light she made out a big, bulky shadow beside the cot where the baby slept.

Connor.

She stilled. She hadn't expected to find him here. Stupid. Of course he'd want to say good-night to the baby. Her anger at him was overtaken by the slow pound of her heart that was suddenly loud in her ears.

Connor turned his head. "The big guy is fast asleep."

"I know, I put him down." Victoria felt the smile tug at the corner of her lips. "Tonight was a struggle, he fought so hard against sleep."

"Tough fellow."

Stopping beside Connor, she said softly, "He's so little."

"And amazingly resilient."

"And we're responsible for him."

"I still find it tough to believe that we're now standing in loco parentis." Connor gazed down at the baby with an expression Victoria could not decipher.

In the place of his parents.

It brought home the reality of the responsibility facing them. And how permanent the arrangement was. It was vital for her and Connor to work together. For all intents and purposes they were now Dylan's parents. The only difference between them was that she really was Dylan's mother.

Her baby lay so still in the crib that she leant forward to touch him.

"He's sleeping—I checked, too." Connor gave her a slight smile. Then his gaze dropped and grew warm.

Victoria glanced down, to find that her dressing gown tie had come undone and fallen open to reveal the white lace, diaphanous nightgowns that she favored.

She flushed. "I think I'll call it a night."

And when Connor responded, "That's a very good idea." She had no idea what to make of his reply.

Eight

"Truce?" Connor offered at breakfast on Saturday.

After a moment Victoria took the hand he held out. This was the closest Connor would come to an apology for employing Anne without her input. "Truce," she agreed.

For Dylan's sake.

And for her own. She had to learn to get on with Connor better. But it wasn't easy—he could be so dominating.

"Anne's very good with Dylan," she conceded. She felt the day brighten when Connor grinned at her.

"Let's take Dylan out today to celebrate his recovery," he suggested as he reached for a slice of toast.

"Today?"

Dismayed, Victoria stared at him. She'd intended to wash her hair while Dylan had his morning nap. The week had sped past, and between work and Dylan she'd hardly had a moment to call her own. She hadn't even had an opportunity to try out the large bath with jets in the guest en suite bathroom.

Connor's face hardened. "I'll take him to the zoo alone—and you can go to work."

Annoyance ignited within her. This was his idea of a truce? "I had no intention of working this weekend. And the zoo sounds fantastic. I just wanted an hour to—" washing her hair sounded so self-indulgent and would no doubt unleash more contempt "—to take a shower."

"How about I feed Dylan and keep him out of your hair for an hour and we leave a little later?"

"That would be wonderful." She beamed at Connor, her heart lighter than it had been for weeks. "Thank you."

Two lionesses lolled about on their backs like giant kittens on a grassy hillock, revealing creamy tummies to the delighted crowd that had taken advantage of the sunny day to visit the zoo.

Dylan gurgled in his pushchair and several children shrieked as one of the lionesses rolled over lithely and rose to her feet, before padding to the edge of the moat that divided the big cats from the spectators.

After the giant feline had finished drinking and had flopped down on a sunny rock, Connor and Victoria meandered farther along the path, Connor pushing the baby's loaded buggy, to where two elephants picked at a hay net with their trunks.

Connor glanced over at Victoria. Since they'd gotten to the zoo she'd attracted a fair amount of second looks. With her hair as sleek and shiny in the sunlight as polished mahogany and her hazel eyes alight with excitement, she looked happier than he'd ever seen her.

And, dammit, she was downright gorgeous.

To get his attention off the way her white denim skirt clung to her posterior, Connor swept Dylan out of his pushchair and held him high.

"See the elephants, Dylan?" Victoria pointed and her buttoned yellow cardigan pulled taut across her breasts.

Connor stifled a groan and his hands involuntarily tightened on the baby, who muttered a protest and wriggled in Connor's arms.

"Sorry, mate."

But Dylan had already stilled at the sight of the huge pachyderms as the nearest elephant flapped its ears. A chortle escaped—the sound of baby delight.

Connor laughed aloud and his eyes caught Victoria's over Dylan's head. For a second they shared a pure joy. Then Dylan began to bump up and down in Connor's arms in excitement.

"Whoa, that's an elephant, Dyl. He's too big to pick a fight with."

"Size doesn't matter," said Victoria.

Connor shot her a glance. Nope, she wouldn't hold back against a bigger opponent.

High color flagged her cheeks. "Sorry, that came out wrong. What I meant to say was that Dylan should never let himself be intimidated."

His mouth twitching, Connor cocked his head to one side and considered her. "So you're conceding size does count?"

She gave him a quick up-down look and Connor waited for the acid comeback. Instead he encountered eyes filled with flustered nervousness.

He'd unsettled her. Score to him.

Connor grinned inwardly.

She blinked rapidly. "I'm just saying the giant doesn't always win—remember David and Goliath."

He swept his gaze slowly over her. "You don't look like any David I've ever met."

She made a sound of mock disgust. Connor threw back his head and laughed, and a moment later, to his astonishment, Victoria joined in.

He held out a hand to her. "Let's go see the otters."

To his surprise she reached for his hand, her fingers linking through his, the pushchair trailing in her other hand. Heat bolted through him and all laughter vanished as he looked at her—*really* looked at her—with a shaken sense of never having seen her before.

Then Dylan butted him, claiming his attention, and Connor came back to reality with a thump.

Later Victoria helped Connor lay a rug down on the freshly mown grass in front of an empty bandstand near a lake with ducks and swans. Connor rolled on his back, pulling Dylan onto his chest while Victoria knelt beside him and reached for the picnic basket they'd brought along.

It was all so domestic.

And most amazing of all, she and Connor hadn't argued once.

He was holding Dylan above him on outstretched arms, making airplane noises. Laughter lines crinkled his cheeks. God, he was gorgeous.

An unwanted echo of that moment when their eyes had locked—of the scintillating awareness that had sizzled earlier—sent a frisson through her.

No.

She was not falling into that trap. Connor was her coguardian, not a prospective date. She daren't start finding him attractive.

Looking away, she rummaged into the basket and pulled out a container of sandwiches that Moni had prepared.

The thud on her back took her breath away. Her eyes shot open in time to see a football rolling along the blanket and a pair of sneakers following in swift pursuit. Boyish hands scooped the ball up.

"Jordan, apologize at once!"

"Sorry." A sheepish grin appeared from beneath a baseball cap. "Won't do it again." A singsong note of overuse underlay the words.

Her breath back, Victoria suppressed the urge to call him a name—or worse, grin at him and condone the carelessness. "Perhaps kick the ball the other way."

Connor sat up beside her, perching Dylan on his knee, and gave the boy a level stare.

"No, I've already told Jordan that he's not to lose a fifty-dollar ball in the tiger's cage." A harried-looking woman with red hair standing up in spikes had appeared. "You have to be more careful, boy."

But Jordan was already gone, zigzagging over the lawn, dribbling the ball ahead of him.

"Kids." The woman rolled her eyes. Then she added, "At least yours is still harmless. Enjoy him while you can. It gets worse."

Victoria started to correct the redhead, to tell her that Dylan wasn't their baby. Then she stopped herself. It was just too hard to explain.

So she smiled instead. "We will."

"Your baby's very cute."

Dylan gurgled and blew a raspberry on cue.

"Thanks."

Jordan's mother shifted her attention to Connor. "He's going to have his mother's goldy-brown eyes and his father's dimples."

"I'm sure you're right," Connor said politely.

Victoria could've kissed him for silently standing by her decision to say as little as possible.

Victoria had laughed with Suzy in the past when complete strangers had told short, blonde, bubbly Suzy how much the newborn Dylan looked like her—not realizing he didn't possess any of Suzy's DNA. Now the memory made her ache with loneliness.

"I'd better find Jordan before he wrecks the place." The redhead scanned the surroundings until she found her son. "Or lands in the pond with the goldfish!" She gave them a rueful smile. "I made the mistake of having only one—so when he doesn't have a friend, guess who has to play with him?" She thrust a thumb at her chest. "Me. Don't do what I did. Make sure you have another kid to keep yours company."

Victoria fidgeted, uncomfortably hot at the too-tempting idea of creating a baby with Connor. Thankfully, Jordan's mother didn't seem to expect a reply; she simply wiggled her fingers at Dylan before vanishing in Jordan's wake.

After what seemed an age Victoria couldn't bear the tingling silence any longer. Unable to help herself, she turned her head. And instantly wished she'd resisted the lure.

Connor was staring at her with predatory speculation, and the normally cool eyes simmered with heat.

Her heart skipped a beat.

Victoria pulled herself together. It was up to her to defuse this sexual tension, and as rapidly as possible.

She chose to do so with humor. "Poor Jordan. What on earth is his mother going to tell his girlfriends one day?"

Connor flung his head back and laughed. And the strange, heavy ache below her heart expanded, filling her with a yearning she'd never expected.

The day ended all too soon.

After securing Dylan in the backseat, Connor held the Maserati's passenger door open for Victoria. And found himself staring at her legs with all the frustrated hunger of a university student eager for his first lay.

They were nice legs. Encased in opaque winter stockings, they were shapely, too. So why the hell hadn't he noticed them before?

Probably because he'd never seen them. She usually wore

black trousers, or long skirts in neutral colors. Black, navy or gray. She never wore a denim skirt that rode up.

Like now.

But he shouldn't feel this…desperate…about stroking them.

She cleared her throat. "You can shut the door."

Caught.

"Sorry." He shook his head sheepishly. "Don't know what I was thinking."

She gave him an old-fashioned look. He shrugged and decided to try for some damage control. He didn't need her knowing how she'd tied him into damned Gordian knots. "So I've always been a bit of a leg man—blame a male's basic instincts."

"Control those instincts." But she laughed, flushing a little. "You've spent too long around the animals today, I think."

"Perhaps," he conceded.

If she only knew how much testosterone her spontaneous smile and slender body had unleashed, she'd be running for the hills—with him in hot pursuit.

He closed the door with a snap and strode around to the driver's side.

A stolen sideways glance revealed that despite Dylan's inquisitive fingers her hair was still sleek. Yet sometime during the day she'd lost the faint tension that always seemed to cling to her. It must be the fact that a smile had never been far from her lips.

It wasn't something she did often enough.

He fired up the Maserati and pulled out onto the road. "Tired?" he asked as he stopped for a red light.

"Exhausted."

He pushed the gearshift into neutral and turned his head. "At least I'm not alone in that."

The smile she gave him caused his groin to tighten.

"But it was worth it," she said. "Thanks. It was a great idea."

Connor told himself to keep it light. "Zoos were created for adults."

She tilted her head. "Why do you say that?"

"Didn't you notice the amount of newborns and young babies? All those parents have been waiting years to legitimately get back into a zoo, bitterly regretting the day they told their parents that thirteen made them too cool for kiddie outings."

She laughed.

Then she ruined his pleasure by pointing out, "The lights have changed."

"Thanks." Connor put the car into gear and accelerated smoothly away.

"You could be right. I think most of the parents there today were having more fun than the kids." She leaned her head back on the headrest. "Dylan certainly slept through a good part of the day."

And it had been during those spells that he'd been tempted to give in to the devilish urge to kiss her. Hot memories of the last time he'd kissed her—when she'd almost ended up totally naked on his lap—had kept him awake more than one night since she'd moved in. But he'd resisted it, fearing he might destroy the delicate truce that had developed between them.

"I had fun," he murmured finally.

"Me, too."

Her voice was smiling. Connor wished he could take his eyes from the road to study her, to see if the corners of her mouth had tipped up into that irresistible curve.

Okay, he wanted her. There. He'd admitted it. He wanted to soak himself in the scent of her, wanted to sate himself in her body.

So where did that leave him?

Connor started through the options with relentless efficiency. He would have to invest time in this—Victoria wouldn't accept anything less, he was certain of that.

Yet he couldn't possibly have an affair with Dylan's co-guardian. Somewhere down the line it would all turn to custard, and Dylan would be the one to suffer.

He thought back to earlier in the afternoon when Jordan's mother had mistaken them for a couple. And Dylan for his baby...

It didn't mean a thing.

Because she'd also assumed Victoria was Dylan's mother.

A glance in the rearview mirror showed Dylan snoozing in the backseat of the Maserati, his dark-gray eyes closed, his cheeks pink and his mouth open in an O.

Goldy-brown eyes. The woman was a kook.

Victoria bore no resemblance to Dylan at all. They weren't even related. But they could be...if he married her.

Because then she'd be the wife of Dylan's sperm-donor father.

He tightened his hands around the steering wheel. God, how had this gotten so complicated? It made his head go numb.

But not nearly as badly as the desire that made him crave to get Victoria into his bed, under his body—

"We should do it again sometime."

"What?" His voice went rough with want. Could she have read his carnal thoughts?

"Visit the zoo again."

Of course she couldn't read his thoughts. He blew out in relief. "Yes, yes, we must."

He could marry her—the crazy thought leapt back into his mind and just as quickly he banished it. He didn't want to marry the woman. Hell, he hadn't wanted to marry Dana, either. Victoria was just as career-minded—nothing like the kind of woman he wanted to live with for the rest of his life.

Except his libido refused to agree.

* * *

After putting the baby into his night suit on Sunday night, Victoria settled down to feed him his bottle in the spacious rocking chair that had been delivered to the nursery yesterday while they'd been out at the zoo.

Yesterday.

She glanced across to Connor where he sat perched on the love seat opposite her, riffling through a pile of picture books on the floor in front of him.

Yesterday she'd discovered a side to Connor that she'd never known existed. A warm, fun, *funny* side. But as soon as they'd gotten home Connor had disappeared, and today she'd barely seen him. She was starting to think he must be avoiding her.

Yet here he was acting as though everything was normal.

Victoria decided she'd never fathom the man out.

He seemed impervious to her disquiet as he picked up a picture book and held it up, saying, "This one, don't you think, big guy?"

Dylan sucked more fiercely on the bottle.

"Good taste, son."

Connor flipped open the first page. Despite his deep voice, he read with a soft, easy rhythm that was curiously soothing. By the time he'd reached the end of the board book, Dylan's eyelids had fallen and Victoria was feeling easier…almost sleepy.

Setting the book on the pile beside the love seat, Connor stretched his arms above his head. "I've been thinking."

The warm, fuzzy feeling receded. Victoria opened her eyes in time to see him rise to his feet. She regarded him warily as tension zapped through her. "About?"

He looked remote, powerful and somewhat alien, standing across from her with his hands on his hips. Was he about to tell her that he'd reconsidered their unconventional custody arrangement—that she should go home? Or was he going to demand she give up work to stay home with Dylan? She'd been dreading that.

She told herself Connor couldn't force her to do anything she didn't want to do.

But imperceptibly her muscles grew taut.

He hesitated only for an instant. "I think we should get married."

"What?"

Dylan stirred in her arms and she rocked him hurriedly. "Where did that come from?" she whispered fiercely to Connor.

"It will make it much easier for Dylan," he said in a low voice, crossing the space between them and staring down at the baby who slept so peacefully in the crook of her arm. "And do away with the constant need for explanations."

"This is because of the woman at the zoo yesterday?"

He spread his hands out wide. "Her mistake was understandable and it's going to happen more and more, particularly if we're living together."

Victoria couldn't believe she hadn't blurted out *no* to his proposal straight away. Until a few days ago there'd always been hostile tension between them. They'd never gotten along, and she'd spent two years actively avoiding him while Suzy and Michael were alive.

So why hadn't she simply said *no?*

One word.

No…no…no!

Easy.

But she didn't say it.

Because of Dylan.

She tilted her head back and studied Connor critically. He was tall. Strong. Deep in her belly, heat stirred. She suppressed it ruthlessly. She knew he was good at sport. He'd be able to pass those skills on to Dylan.

Dylan was the only reason she could ever marry Connor….

A glance down at the baby revealed his smooth, round face, untroubled by the demons chasing her. If she married Connor then Dylan would have a family again. A mother and a father. A world away from merely living with his guardians.

How could she deprive him of that?

A real family.

But Victoria couldn't lie to herself. There was another, much more selfish reason to marry Connor. If she did her place in Dylan's life would be secure.

She would be able to relax, to stop worrying that he'd get rid of her as soon as Dylan settled down. As his wife, it would be a lot harder for Connor to evict her from Dylan's life.

Uncannily, Connor echoed her thoughts: "If we were married we could provide a stable home for Dylan."

A shivery awareness filled her. How far did he intend to take this idea of giving Dylan a stable home? She thought about the frank woman at the zoo. Don't do what I did. Make sure you have another kid to keep yours company. Would Connor want to provide Dylan with siblings? Would he expect her to make love with him? Past experience had proved that he only had to touch her for desire to ignite into burning heat.

She turned her attention away from the baby and back to the man who'd taken over her thoughts, her life. "Connor—"

He held up a hand. "Wait. Before you reject the idea, you need to know that I'm committed to this. I won't pull out in a year or two and want a divorce."

She tried to read the expression in his eyes, but the night-light was too dim.

To put a little distance between them she rose to her feet and gently deposited the snoozing Dylan in his cot. Tugging at the cord that hung near the baby's cot, she flooded the room with soft light and turned to face the man who had put her world into uproar.

"How can you possibly be so sure? You might fall in love

and want a real marriage." Would she be any good at marriage? Her parents had married because she was already on the way. Would marrying for Dylan's sake be any different?

"I'm not looking for love." He gave her a crooked smile. "Let's just say that Dana forever killed any desire I had for a 'real' marriage."

Sadness unexpectedly seeped through Victoria. No woman would be able to steal that cold, shriveled heart. He'd shut himself up behind high, impenetrable walls.

Deeply disappointed for some reason she couldn't fathom, she found herself shaking her head. "I can't marry you."

He seemed to take root and a stillness overtook his large frame. "You don't think it would be a good idea for Dylan?"

What was she supposed to say to that? Tell him about her own parents' failures? And let him realize how poor a mother she might be? Definitely not! "Of course, Dylan would benefit."

"So why not marry me?"

She shifted restlessly. She thought of her father…ever drifting, never home. Of her mother's unhappiness. "There's more to marriage than Dylan."

His eyes gleamed. "Are you referring to sex?"

Her skin went all tight.

"You don't want to have sex with me? Is that it?"

Oh, dear God. He'd misunderstood. But sex…

She couldn't stop staring at him. At the depth of his chest. The large, capable hands. The hard mouth that could smile so gorgeously. Her skin grew tighter. "No…no, I don't."

He smiled. It wasn't a very nice smile. "May I ask why not?"

Damn him.

She wriggled like a bug on a stick. "Because I don't make love with every conceited, arrogant jerk who comes along."

He shook his head and laughed. "That puts me in my place."

"And I don't like you," she said, seized by a burst of unreasonable anger, "and I'm quite sure you don't like me much either."

"Liking has nothing whatsoever to do with sex, Victoria." He drawled her name out slowly, deliberately, making her feel utterly *Victorian* and positively puritanical.

At the pale-silver gleam in those dangerous eyes she grew itchy, but forced herself to sit unmoving. "I need to actually *like* a man to make love with him."

"So naive. You can't have liked a great many men then."

The implication took her breath away. "I'm not a misanthrope—I'm discerning. And it's only you I've never liked. I've made love to enough men to know that I don't do casual encounters."

She'd even dated a guy for two years before breaking it off when he'd asked her to marry him. She'd gotten scared. It would never have worked—not even if she'd been more confident—he'd been easygoing and fun loving. A tumbleweed. He'd constantly nagged her to relax, to slow down, unable to understand that she was driven for reasons of her own to make a success of her life. Whatever the cost.

At least that was one thing she had in common with Connor—he'd worked hard to get where he was. Even though he'd expected her to take extended leave at the drop of a hat.

Shadows flickered in the silvery depths. "There will be nothing casual about our encounter. I can promise you that."

She shivered deep inside. "You make it sound dangerous."

He stalked closer. "We've always struck sparks off each other, and this will be no different." He stared into her eyes, searching for something she was equally determined never to concede. "It will blow your world apart."

It was so tempting….

"I know there's no one out there waiting for you. Just say yes, Victoria."

Too tempting.

And the emptiness would be forever filled by Connor... and Dylan. A family. A chance to have what Suzy had had. What she'd never dared hope for.

Before she could think better of it, she leaned forward and placed her lips against his.

He froze.

She parted her lips. Lightly, delicately she traced her tongue tip over his mouth. His chest lifted against her, rising, pressing against breasts that were suddenly tender.

She tasted him, sipped at him, until his breath escaped in short, jerky gasps. His arms came around her, engulfing her, holding her close. He was hard, all male. The snug fit of his jeans couldn't hide the erection that had sprung to life, a rock-like ridge against her lower belly.

He cupped her bottom, pulled her up against him and took her mouth. It was her turn to shudder with desire. He thrust his tongue deep, and the act of possession sent a primitive thrill through her.

Stroking the inside of her mouth, his tongue searched out the smooth skin inside her cheeks, the highly sensitized roof-arch.

She groaned, a hoarse, wanting sound.

No longer aware of where they were—barely aware of how long it had been since the kiss began—she focused on the hunger that raged between them.

He moved closer, his leg pushing between hers, the harsh fabric of his jeans rough against her skin. But that was sexy, too.

Until Dylan mumbled in the cot behind her and she leapt away from Connor as if she'd been scalded.

Connor stood rigid. His eyes were wide and, for the first time since the night he'd come to tell her of Michael's death, she recognized the emotion in his eyes.

Shock.

Her heart hammering, she balled her hands at her sides to

stop them from reaching for him. "See what you made me do? That was monumentally stupid."

He swallowed, and she fixed her gaze on his Adam's apple, watched it bob up and down, avoiding his too-astute eyes. Hurriedly she added, "*You* irritated *me*." And flicked her gaze up.

Then wished she hadn't.

White-hot. That's what his eyes were. Enough to incinerate her.

"I overreacted—and so did you." Silence. "Don't you agree?" More silence. "I don't want to make love without it meaning anything," she protested, more to convince herself than him, wishing she wasn't having this wretched one-sided conversation with a man she simply didn't understand.

"I'm not asking you to." He sounded so reasonable. "I only asked you to marry me."

Her heart sank. "So you're proposing a marriage in name only? Absolutely no sex?" She risked a look at him. His expression was indecipherable.

"Do I understand you correctly?" He drew a deep, audible breath. "If we take sex out of the equation you'd marry me?"

"Maybe…" It was a croak of sound. But her body was urging *more, more, more*.

"This is no time for maybe, Victoria. Yes or no?"

They weren't touching. Yet over the gap that separated them she could feel the heat of his body, the force of his power.

Victoria started to tremble. She was ready to say anything to stop the sizzle.

"Yes," she sighed.

Nine

Connor discovered over the next few days that getting married solely for Dylan's sake wasn't what he wanted. He wasn't that noble. He wanted more.

She was driving him crazy. Once or twice as she sashayed past he considered yanking her off her feet, into his lap, and repeating the experiment.

Their no-sex agreement had to be the most idiotic thing he'd ever done. Hell, she was going to wear his ring. That would brand her his for the world to see. Yet he wouldn't be allowed to touch. Sooner or later something was going to have to give—and it would be Victoria. He was quite confident that he would achieve that. She would come around. He'd see to it because he sure as hell had no intention of sticking to their stupid pact.

In the meantime, he made up for it by looking. Surreptitiously, carefully and at every opportunity he got.

It was torture.

Several times each day he would call Victoria at work—ostensibly to talk about Dylan. But he found himself looking forward to those segments of time when her husky voice came over the line, especially when he managed to get her to laugh.

Lust had turned him into something pathetic.

It was a sign of how entangled he'd become with his new life that, when Iris came into his spacious corner office with his coffee and announced that she'd heard Dana and Paul were getting married, Connor felt one brief flare of resentment and then…nothing.

The lack of turmoil and emotion was liberating. He stood staring at Iris until she said, "Connor, are you okay?"

He gave his assistant an unabashed grin. "I'm better than okay—I'm great."

She snorted. "Because Dana and Paul are getting married?"

"Yep." His grin widened. "Makes me feel much better than I thought."

A wave of relief crashed over him that there was no need for anger, or to exact further revenge. That phase of his life was over.

What he had now was so much better.

Iris straightened the papers on his desk into a neat pile. "There's a rumor that Dana's pregnant."

Even that didn't disturb him. He grinned at her over the top of the coffee mug. "I should've anticipated that. Poor Paul."

"You had a lucky escape."

"I certainly did." Setting the mug down on a wooden coaster, he tipped his head sideways and studied Iris as she slit his correspondence with a letter opener. "You never indicated you didn't like Dana."

"Wasn't my place—you seemed happy enough with her."

His gaze paused on her pursed mouth. "You're not the only one. Michael never liked her, either, nor did Brett." His brother had been open in his reservations about Dana after their first meeting. Of course, Dana hadn't cared for Brett either—she'd been relieved that he lived in London.

There was a scrape as Iris shredded the empty envelopes. "Dana was always good at her job, and she knew who to impress. But she'd clamber over anyone in her way to get what she wanted." Iris turned back to face him.

Leaning back in his executive chair, Connor folded his arms behind his head. "It wasn't easy for her. People are always harder on women who are successful in business." He thought of Victoria. "Even me." He couldn't help wondering what Iris would make of Victoria.

"It had nothing to do with Dana's successes, just the way she went about achieving them." Disapproval came off Iris in waves. "And you shouldn't be defending her." With that, she bustled out of his office, pausing at the doorway to say, "Don't forget you have a meeting at noon."

Connor nodded, then swiveled his chair to look out the window at the knot of gum trees that flourished beside a pond. A pair of ungainly blue-and-black pukekos minced on orange webbed feet along the bank of the pond, picking for food.

His motherly assistant thought Dana had used him as a way to get what she'd wanted, but to be honest, he'd used Dana, too. He was starting to realize that what he liked about Dana was that she *didn't* affect him—he could stay heart whole and devoted to work. He didn't think about her all day long. He hadn't felt the same compulsion to talk to her as he did with Victoria. Dana hadn't been a constant distraction from his work. Sure, she'd been a very decorative diversion, and of course he'd gotten a kick out the covetous looks other men had given her. And she could be as feral as a sex-starved mink in bed.

Yet her infidelity still left a bitter taste.

But Michael had hit the nail on the head. It had been his

pride—rather than his heart—that had been bleeding when she'd walked out.

He'd never thought he'd land himself in a similar position.

Yet Victoria was even sexier to him, and her beauty was more subtle but no less captivating…and he had a suspicion that Victoria could make him never want to go to work again.

And she was even smarter than Dana.

Just look how she'd gotten him to agree to a marriage without sex—only minutes after kissing him stupid. She'd reduced him to a quivering lump.

Masterly.

And he'd been the fool who'd agreed to it! Even though he was certain he'd be able to convince her otherwise. Given time.

As the pukekos disappeared into the reeds on the water-line, an inner voice whispered, Dana would never have done that. She'd have used sex as another weapon in her arsenal.

But then he couldn't remember ever wanting, yearning, going mad with desire for Dana in quite the same way….

Out of respect for Suzy and Michael it was decided the wedding would be a small one with no frills and flounces—and definitely no fairy-tale white dress.

The following night after they'd put Dylan to bed Connor came to the small sitting room upstairs that Victoria had claimed as her own, where he hadn't invaded until now. He paused at the threshold, and she watched him survey the changes she'd made to the elegant cream-and-dull-gold décor. The addition of a wall hanging in muted colors that she'd brought from her town house. A large fern she'd called Audrey, which was draping enthusiastic fronds over the back of the couch where she sat holding a wineglass.

"I don't want to disturb you," he said at last.

Didn't the man know by now that he always disturbed

her? Even wearing only a T-shirt and black jeans he managed to make her pulse pick up.

Of course she'd never admit it.

"Would you like a glass of burgundy?" she asked, setting her glass down and reaching for a clean one from the butler's tray on the side of the couch. "A client gave it to me—and it's rather good." Relaxing, too—which she needed now that the realization she and Connor were actually getting married was starting to sink in.

Connor looked taken aback for a moment, then nodded. "Just half a glass. I'm not staying long."

Once she'd poured, he moved farther into the room. Taking the glass from her, he raised it to his nose before sniffing and saying, "Mmm…nice." Then he glanced down at her. "I came to ask for a list of friends and family you're inviting to the wedding. Iris—my PA—will send out invitations if you give me details. She's a whiz."

"No."

That caused his eyebrows to leap to his hairline. "Aren't you a little busy to be doing it yourself?"

"There isn't anyone I want to invite." Victoria took a sip of her wine. "Have a taste, it's very smooth."

Settling himself against the antique writing desk across from her, he sipped. "Very smooth. No friends at all?"

She shook her head slowly, supremely conscious of the weight of his stare.

With the exception of Suzy, she'd lost contact with most of her friends over the past ten years, too busy with work. Occasionally she'd gone out with Suzy and her teacher friends to a movie, or to dinner with a group from Archer, Cameron & Edge. But she wasn't close to any of them.

"What about family?" He shifted, crossing one ankle over the other where he leaned, the rustle of denim loud in the intimacy of the sitting room. "My brother's coming."

"I don't have brothers or sisters." Victoria dropped her gaze away. "My mom's dead, and I haven't spoken to my father in years."

"Then this might be the time to invite him and mend some fences. Both my parents are dead—at least you still have a father who could be there for you."

She played with the stem of her glass. Connor couldn't know what he was asking of her. "I thought the purpose of the day was to get married and provide a family for Dylan."

"Nothing wrong with using the opportunity for reconciliation, Victoria."

Connor's arrogant assumption that inviting her tumbleweed father to her wedding would make amends for decades of irresponsibility and selfish neglect rubbed her the wrong way. "So I take it you'll be inviting Dana and Paul?"

There was a horrible pause. Then he said, "Okay, maybe we should just focus on the wedding."

"Good idea." In an effort to restore the peace she said brightly, "I didn't know you had a brother."

He drained his glass and set it down on the desk behind him. "Brett's been living it up in London for the past few years."

"And he's coming all the way out to New Zealand?"

Straightening, Connor gave her a grim smile. "It's my wedding—probably the only one he'll ever see me celebrate. Of course he's coming."

Less than a week after Connor had asked Victoria to marry him, the wedding took place.

In sharp contrast to Suzy and Michael's wedding, it was a small affair with no bouquets, flower girls or white lacy bridal dress in sight. In fact, Victoria decided that *celebrate* was a far too strong word for the civil ceremony that they rushed through in an anonymous Queen Street government building.

Afterward, accompanied by Connor's brother and Anne—who'd come to take care of Dylan but ended up acting as a witness—they went to a lovely restaurant set in the rolling, parklike gardens of Auckland's domain. Sitting at a table on a verandah that overlooked a series of lakes shaded by budding willows and frequented by swans, Victoria's gaze settled on Dylan perched in the high chair beside Anne, and she finally relaxed.

Married.

Her place in Dylan's life was secure now.

"Congratulations!" Connor's brother waved a glass of champagne. "Welcome to our family."

Victoria smiled and raised her glass. Brett's personality had come as a surprise. Younger than Connor, he had a boyish flirtatiousness that made her laugh.

"Connor needs to be married," he told her while Connor discussed their meal with the restaurant owner. "Even though I would rather you'd had a very unequivocal, big, splashy wedding instead of this hole-in-the-corner affair."

"*Needs* to be married?" Victoria raised one brow skeptically and carefully ignored the rest of his explosive statement.

"Oh, yes. He likes domesticity."

"*Connor?*"

She glanced at the man whose commanding presence had conjured up the owner and a trio of waiters in minutes. His baby brother was mistaken—Connor was as domesticated as a Bengal tiger.

Brett nodded emphatically. "Oh, yes. He's suffering from empty nest syndrome."

She must have looked blank, because Brett elaborated. "Since I left home." His eyes widened. "He never told you that he raised me?"

"No."

Victoria started to feel ridiculous. She knew nothing

about the man she was marrying—except that he'd been dumped by his girlfriend and betrayed by his partner two years ago, and had built a multimillion dollar corporation out of the ruins of those relationships. She'd been crazy to think that was enough. "Until last week I didn't even know he had a brother."

"What mischief are you whispering to my bride?"

The owner had departed, wearing a very satisfied smile. But Connor's eyes narrowed alarmingly as he focused on Victoria and his brother.

"No mischief…yet. I'm still trying to impress her with how upstanding we are. I'll get to the skeletons in the closet later."

Connor's eyes crinkled into a smile. "Those are all yours, brother."

After that lunch became a noisy, happy affair—where even Dylan contributed much gurgling. The food was sublime and the pale-golden sunshine gave the occasion luster. After listening to the brothers bantering, Victoria met Anne's eyes and both women collapsed in paroxysms of laughter.

Dylan finally decided he'd had enough sitting.

"I'll show him the swans," Anne said, rising to free the baby from the high chair. "And it's probably time for a change, too."

"I'll get a travel rug from the car—" Connor was on his feet "—for you to lay him on."

"You may have noticed that Connor doesn't talk much about himself," Brett said to Victoria once Connor had disappeared around the corner of the building.

Now, that was an understatement. She flashed Brett a wry glance.

"Our parents are dead—did you know that?"

She nodded. "He mentioned it, but he didn't give any details." And she hadn't asked because the last thing she'd wanted was Connor asking questions about her estrangement from her father.

"A train crash." Brett paused. "That's why he was so upset about Michael. Brought back old memories."

She hadn't even known; Connor had hidden the old, festering wound so well under that icy exterior.

Brett leaned closer. "Has he told you about Dana?"

"His ex?"

"The viper."

A giggle escaped despite Victoria's attempts to look disapproving. "Brett!"

"She kicked him out of his own home, but in a way it was a relief when I heard. I was scared shitless Connor would marry her—she was angling for it."

"Should you be telling the new wife all this stuff?"

"It's on a need-to-know basis." He dipped down close and lowered his voice conspiratorially. "Dana is poison. She told Connor she wanted children, but he didn't believe her."

Despite her qualms, Victoria couldn't resist probing for more information. It was unlikely to be forthcoming from Connor. "Why?"

"He thought her work meant too much for her to take time out for kids."

Uh-oh. That went some way toward explaining his attitude in relation to Dylan with her. "How do you know all this?"

He sat back in his chair and selected a toothpick. "I watched…and they sniped at each other sometimes. And after they split up Connor came to London and I took him on a pub crawl."

Victoria frowned.

"Think of it as therapy—it was the only way I could get him to talk."

"You're devious."

"Very," he said with immense satisfaction. "And you'd better remember that, because I'm counting on you to feather Connor's nest and keep him happy."

Victoria laughed at the outrageous comment. But the sound dried in her throat when a hand landed on her waist. "Be careful of my baby brother."

Connor's husky growl close to her right ear caused her to shiver with delight.

"He's just been warning me of how dangerous he is." She slanted a mirthful look up at Connor.

Resting his arms across the back of her chair, he leaned closer, his body warm and his male scent familiar. Shuddery sensations of awareness tingled over her nape as her new groom said, "Unfortunately, it's all true."

"Right."

"See, I told you to be careful of me." Brett looked as innocent as an angel. "Now I'm off to whisper some secrets to Dylan."

"More like flirt with Anne," Connor murmured as Brett took off down to the water. He slid into the chair that Brett's desertion had freed.

The latent tension in Victoria wound a notch tighter. No longer laughing, she pivoted on her seat to face Connor. "Brett tells me you brought him up."

"He exaggerates."

"So how old was he when your parents died?"

"You mean he didn't get around to telling you everything?" The humor vanished, and his eyes cooled, becoming remote.

"He ran out of time. But I deserve to know—I'm your wife, remember?"

"In name only."

The terse retort came like a slap in the face and she looked down, determined he shouldn't see how he had wounded her.

"Brett was fifteen."

Victoria snatched up the olive branch. Driven by an overwhelming need to know more about him, she lifted her chin and asked, "And you were?"

"Twenty-two."

"Twenty-two! That would have been a demanding time of your life."

Connor didn't say anything.

"It was good of you to look after him," she persisted.

"Anyone would have done it."

"No, they wouldn't." Her father had shown next to no responsibility for his wife and child. Yet Connor had single-handedly raised his brother. She studied his guarded features, admiring the purpose and determination in the rocklike jaw, the sweep of the wide cheekbones and the dark hair that the late August wind had ruffled, giving him a sexy, rumpled look. "And now you're doing it again. For Dylan."

He shrugged. "Michael was my friend—my best friend, as it turned out."

Without the irony, she might never have asked, "Tell me about your business partner."

"Brett talk about Paul, too?"

"No."

"So what brought on this bout of curiosity?"

His gaze was unnerving. Victoria gave a careless shrug and reached for her sunglasses. "Perhaps I'm just trying to understand what would drive a man's friend to behave like that."

"You think I drove him to do it?"

"I didn't say that!" She blew out a breath in frustration. "I think what he did to you was despicable."

"And what do you think of Dana's behavior?"

She met his gaze squarely. "I thought that was pretty shabby, too."

He nodded slowly as though her answer had satisfied a question deep inside him. Then, pinning her with his intimidating gaze, he said, "I once heard you tell Suzy that you didn't blame Dana one bit."

Victoria slipped her sunglasses on, and frowned. "I said that? When?"

"The day that we first met. You called me a jerk."

Her eyes went around behind the dark lenses. "You *heard* that?"

"So you remember."

"Yes, I was furious with you for attacking Suzy." And it would have knifed him when he was already down. "So that's why you were so hostile to me at the wedding."

"Partly."

She'd thought he'd taken an unreasonable dislike to her, and that had hurt. To learn that her own behavior had been a major part of the problem made her want to groan in dismay. "I'd found out while I was away on a grueling weeklong audit that Suzy was getting married. I was concerned about Suzy." She paused, then decided he deserved the whole truth. "I was dog tired and your in-your-face arrogance was more than I could stomach." Of course she'd bristled in return and the whole sorry situation had snowballed.

"And the other part of your hostility? Where did that come from," she asked, curious now.

"It's complicated."

He was a complicated man. She decided to humor him, make him laugh. She shifted her chair back a little. "Come on, how complicated can it be? You're a male, men are supposed to be easy."

"I am definitely easy," he deadpanned.

Victoria rolled her eyes. "You're not getting out of this conversation by relying on sexual innuendo."

"I wanted to see you blush so deliciously again."

"I don't blush." She felt the rush of color even as he quirked a dark brow at her.

"That was so much easier than I thought," he murmured, his eyes full of lazy humor.

"Oh, stop it!" She didn't know where to look. He was altogether overwhelming in this mood. "Tell me the other reason you disliked me."

"You reminded me of Dana."

Her breath caught. Ouch. All relaxation and lazy desire fled. "I would *never* do what she did to you."

She turned as Brett and Anne came up the grassy back toward them, Dylan happily squealing in Brett's arms. "Don't confuse me with Dana, Connor—I'm nothing like her."

"Sure," said Connor from behind her.

But he sounded far from convinced.

Silence fell over the house.

Victoria had discarded the pale-ivory suit she'd worn for the wedding, and showered. Anne had long since left for home, and Brett had taken off to meet the old friends he was staying with. Victoria set the empty baby bottle on a table beside her, Dylan having been lulled to sleep by Connor's reading. She looked over the baby's sleeping head to where Connor lay sprawled on the dark-blue carpet at the foot of the rocker, his head propped up on his elbow…watching her.

She shifted, and the nursing chair rocked in a gentle motion.

"Is the baby getting heavy?"

"A little," Victoria prevaricated, taking the easy excuse he offered for her sudden restlessness.

Connor pushed himself to his feet in one lithe movement. "I'll put him to bed." His eyes sought hers. "Then we can go downstairs and share a toast to our marriage."

Butterflies fluttered in her stomach at the thought of being alone with Connor. "Oh, he's fine—"

But it was too late. Connor had already swept Dylan up. For an instant the emptiness in her arms roused an ache of separation and she felt a flare of anxiety that she might never hold Dylan again.

She shook off the foolish fancy.

There would be lots of time to spend with her baby. She would be here for every day of his life—she could watch him grow, reach out to the world, become a real, rounded person.

Marriage to Connor had ensured that.

And, in spite of their differences in the past, both of them were committed to making this unlikely marriage work.

It had to.

Not only for Dylan, but for them, too.

Pulling her dressing gown more tightly around her, Victoria crossed the room to the oak crib where Connor stood, his broad shoulders accentuated by the white dress shirt, his hips lean in dark pants. She leaned forward as he tucked Dylan in.

"He's getting big. Must be devouring rubber bands." Maternal pride filled her as she studied the length of the oblivious baby. "He's going to be tall one day."

Connor pulled up the patchwork Peter Rabbit quilt. "He's still just a baby. So many hopes and dreams tied up in one little person."

The words moved her. "You feel that way, too?"

He turned his head, and in the dim glow of the nursery lamp part of his face remained in shadow. "I love him."

She hadn't imagined Connor capable of love. He'd always seemed too remote, too self-sufficient. Yet clearly he loved Brett, and now he was telling her that he loved Dylan, too. The tender expression he wore as he glanced down at Dylan made Victoria feel all soft and molten inside.

Connor doesn't talk much about himself, Brett had said earlier. Well, she'd just have to learn how to draw him out, Victoria decided. The man she'd just glimpsed would be worth finding.

* * *

Downstairs the overhead lights in the living room blazed, illuminating the sculpted lines of the wide deck outside and reflecting off the glistening surface of the swimming pool under the night sky beyond.

"What about a glass of champagne?" Connor offered, and Victoria nodded.

He pushed some buttons in a wall panel and the brightness in the room dimmed, immediately transforming the mood from stark sophistication to shadowed intimacy. Victoria came to a dead standstill in the middle of an exquisite kelim and cast him a wary glance.

The invitation had been for a toast, she'd thought—not a seduction.

He extracted a bottle of champagne from a fridge concealed in a mahogany wall unit and two long-stemmed glasses from a cubbyhole above, and came toward Victoria where she stood dithering. Giving her a glass, he took her free hand.

Immediately, conflicting sensations rushed through Victoria. Trepidation. Nerves. And something far too close to desire for her comfort. But instead of fighting to free her hand she let him lead her to the black leather couch, her heartbeat loud in her ears.

"I prefer to sit on the deck outside at night, but it's a little fresh out there tonight." Connor increased her confusion by sinking down beside her instead of choosing the matching couch on the other side of the Murano-glass coffee table. After he'd filled both glasses, he said, "We're paying the price for those open blue skies earlier."

Determined to keep the conversation neutral, she said, "I'm not surprised you spend a lot of time on the deck—the view of the bay is simply stunning."

It had been one of the first things about the house to capture her attention—right then she'd seen what Connor had meant.

With its hardwood floors, big spaces, wide lawns and sparkling pool, this was the ideal place for a boy to grow up.

"And we were fortunate with the glorious weather today," she added when he made no move to touch her. Get a grip, she told herself. They had a deal. She relaxed enough to take a sip of her bubbly wine.

"To my bride."

Victoria couldn't read his expression. The subtle tension notched upward. She decided to take the toast at face value and raised her glass in return. "My groom."

He scooted closer and clinked his glass to hers. A sharp ting rang out. They sipped…and over the rims of the glasses their eyes held.

A bolt of electricity sizzled between them.

Victoria tore her gaze from his.

His hand came up and wrenched the black bow tie from his throat, peeled open the top button of his shirt. Victoria's breath caught as her attention honed in on the ripple of a pulse under the swarthy skin. She didn't dare raise her eyes lest she meet his and be scorched by more shudders of desire.

He shifted beside her. Aware of every inch of his long body, of the coiling muscle of his thighs under his dark, formal pants, Victoria stayed absolutely immobile. He leaned closer, and her breath dried up.

God.

"I should—"

"I think I should—"

They both stopped. Victoria gave an awkward laugh, and fluttered a quick sideways glance at him. "I was going to say I should go to bed…it's been a long day."

"And I was going to say I should kiss my bride," said Connor with wry humor.

"Oh."

She knew he'd seen her alarm because one side of his mouth kicked up.

"I still think I should." He leaned nearer and, when she did nothing, he pressed his lips to hers.

For a long moment there was no sound.

Then he lifted his head. "Not so scary, was it?"

"I wasn't scared," she objected, all too conscious of the hard-edged features and his unblinking silver-gray gaze.

His hand reached out and his fingertips traced her brow bone. "Then why the wide eyes?"

Okay, so maybe she had been scared. Not of him, but of responding too enthusiastically to anything he might try, taking the kiss far beyond the kind of intimacy he intended. Like she did every time he kissed her.

Connor had a knack of making her want…more.

"We agreed no sex. You took me by surprise," she sputtered.

He laughed. "A kiss is a long way from sex."

Now he thought she was prissy. Damn. But she wasn't going to let him roll her over. "It's a darn good start along the road. Our bargain was that I marry you to give Dylan a stable home. No sex involved."

"The billion-dollar baby bargain," he said sardonically, his fingers sliding along her jawline.

"Hey—" the implication annoyed her, and his caress was unsettling "—I'm not doing this for money, you know that. I wouldn't take a cent from you."

But despite her heated words her bones were turning to fluid under his tantalizing touch. The citrus and male scent of him surrounded her. And the assault on her senses conspired to make her give a little shiver.

His fingertips came to rest under her chin. "Perhaps I should've offered you a million dollars to walk away from your custody and guardian responsibilities?"

Could he be serious? She wasn't sure. But she decided to rid him of that notion once and for all. "You're insane. I would never've taken it. Dylan is worth more than any amount of money to me."

"And me, too." He moved his thumb along her throat until it rested in the soft hollow beneath her ear. "Stalemate. So we're stuck with each other."

"But we're not going to have sex." She sounded ridiculously breathless.

He smiled, a slow, wolfish smile. "If you're certain, then why is your pulse beating so fast?"

"It's not my pulse—it's yours you're feeling through your thumb," she said in a strangled voice.

Connor laughed. And her toes curled up at the sound.

"We're going to have sex," he said. "And like I promised, it will be far from casual."

"You're so arrogant," she accused him.

"Think so?"

He moved and she squealed.

"Too late." His arms were around her shoulders. "I'm not going to let you go."

"But we agreed—"

"The idea of being married and not making love is…" His voice trailed away as he placed a kiss against her neck.

"Is what?" He'd taken her breath away again—along with her ability to think.

"It's stupid." His mouth opened hungrily against her silken skin. "Whose idea was it, anyway?"

"I don't know." Her voice was hoarse.

He blew softly, and shivers broke over her skin.

"Million-dollar question—what do you want me to do now, Victoria?"

Was he asking permission? Did Connor really care what she wanted? Or would he just take what he wanted and tumble away, like every man she'd ever known?

Ten

Connor felt her stiffen.

Not giving her time to gather her defenses, he licked the hollow at the base of her throat.

She jumped.

He repeated the caress. This time she groaned, and her body went soft, pliable—no sign of resistance remaining.

Her dressing gown opened with one tug of the sash that she'd tied in a bow. Underneath she wore a white, lacy confection that was likely to drive him insane.

Three buttons teased him.

It took him less than thirty seconds to unfasten them all. He brushed the neckline open, exposing the sweetly scented dip between her breasts. The slopes of her breasts glowed, pale and luminescent. Like a pair of priceless pearls.

Dana had always sported a tan. He forced his thoughts away from Dana, and stroked his hand across the rise of pale skin.

"Beautiful."

He peeled the lace of the tab away, baring her breasts and covered her with his hands. "See? You fit inside my palms like you were made for them. Why would you want more?"

He could feel himself growing hard.

Releasing her, he unbuttoned his shirt and shrugged it off. Her hands came up and touched the bare skin of his stomach. His muscles pulled taut, and he fought back a groan of delight.

He wanted to murmur, "Touch me, touch me". But it was too soon.

Instead he lowered his head and kissed the tips of her exposed breasts.

She arched her back, coming off the couch.

Connor opened his mouth, covering her whole nipple and used his tongue.

Victoria moaned, her eyelashes falling against her cheeks. Her head moved restlessly from side to side.

He moved across and sucked on the other nipple, until she shifted and moaned again.

"Like that?"

All he heard was a guttural sound of pure desire.

Connor blew on both nipples, and watched as they hardened and gooseflesh rippled across her breasts and belly. The hunger that took him was raw and primal in its intensity.

Lifting his own head, Connor slipped his hands under the hem of her skimpy nightgown, and stripped it off over her head.

His fingers trembled with want. And his heart was racing, the beat of it pounding in his ears.

He rose to his feet and dropped his pants and boxers.

"Don't stop," she remonstrated, opening her eyes. They grew wide as they took in his nakedness, his readiness for her.

He waited for her to back out.

But she didn't.

Instead she sat up and stroked the length of his erection

with her delicate fingers. Connor saw stars. He fell back against the couch and pulled her over him.

"Now," he whispered.

She straddled him. Before he could shift himself nearer, she'd surrounded him with her hands and drawn him to the entrance of her body. In one swift movement she sank down on him.

Her body was hot and wet and wild around his.

When she started to move, he moved, too. The rhythm that built was full of passion and power. As he thrust upward, Connor felt the heat take him.

He met her gaze, the green-gold eyes wild with emotion. He'd never seen anything…felt anything…so absolutely, perfectly exquisite.

"I can't hold—" He gasped.

Then pleasure surrounded him as her orgasm hurled her over the edge and the feminine shivers trembled around him.

Victoria awakened to the sound of clinking china. She opened her eyes to the unfamiliar surroundings of Connor's bedroom. And the domestic picture of Connor clasping Dylan—clad in only a diaper—against his hip, while he carefully poured tea. The dark liquid spilled into two delicate, rose-patterned tea cups arranged on a tray on the chest at the bottom of the bed, much to Dylan's wide-eyed fascination.

Connor should've looked incongruous—he didn't.

In fact he'd never looked more gorgeous. Wearing only a pair of boxers—and an almost naked baby—he'd never appeared more male. Her gaze lingered on the broad chest on which she'd rested her head before falling asleep in the early hours of the morning.

Images of the intimacies they'd shared last night flashed through her mind.

It had been wonderful. And, as Connor had promised, there had been nothing casual about the experience. Victoria stretched, languorously, slowly becoming aware of all the hidden places where she ached.

"You're awake," Connor greeted her as she moved.

She gave a soft groan. He raised a dark eyebrow with interest and she felt her cheeks grow hot.

Before he could say anything—anything at all, however innocent—she said, "Oh, I'm dying for a cup of tea."

At his slow grin she realized she'd given him an opening for any number of risqué comments, so she simply cooed at Dylan to break the growing hush.

A moment later Connor asked blandly, "Do you want sugar in your tea?"

The incongruity of it all struck her. She'd slept with a man who knew barely anything about her, who didn't even know how she took her tea. Yet he was her husband—and now he knew exactly what intimacies made her go wild with delight.

As for herself, she suspected she was falling headlong in love with her handsome husband. The thought of being at a man's mercy was what she'd always dreaded. But it was proving to be the most sensual, most emotional experience of her life. Nothing like what her mother had experienced.

"One spoon, please."

He stirred it in. Hitching Dylan higher, he picked up the cup and saucer and came around the bed end.

As Connor put the tea down on the bed stand, Dylan grunted in protest and wriggled in his arms, clearly intent on diving into the covers. Laughing, Victoria hoisted the baby into her arms and buried her nose in his soft neck, making snuffling sounds that caused him to wriggle more wildly. Happiness soared through her.

Dylan grabbed at her hair.

"Ow." Victoria carefully freed his fingers from the silky

strands. Connor stooped forward to help. Dylan, finally spying an opening, dived under Connor's arm in search of the tea cup.

"Hot," Victoria said. Dylan reared away, already recognizing the warning.

A pile of newspapers landed on the bed beside her. "Why don't you take it easy. Drink your tea, and take the opportunity to read the paper?"

She laughed. "Opportunity? With Dylan to help?"

"I'd planned to take Dylan to shower with me."

"Ooh, he'll love that." And she gave Connor a glowing smile. "Thank you. I can't remember when last I relaxed and simply lazed in bed."

Shadows darkened the eyes that looked down into hers. Her heart contracted. They both knew the last time for either of them to relax without a care had been before that watershed weekend when Michael and Suzy had been killed.

Her throat tightened…her happiness, this dizzy emotional roller coaster, had followed the worst tragedy of her life. The terrible, wrenching loss that had taken Suzy from her had given her Dylan—and brought Connor into her life. He was far from being the total jerk she'd always thought he was— she'd discovered a side of him she liked…loved…that she wanted to get to know better.

It was insane.

Connor bent forward and kissed her forehead. "Take it easy, Tory. Dylan and I will make breakfast after our shower." He swept the baby off the covers and jiggled Dylan up and down. "Won't we, big guy?"

At the familiar name, she gave him a misty smile, then settled herself against the pillows and listened to Dylan's crowing with glee.

"Thanks, Connor. It sounds like heaven."

He hesitated. "I seem to remember Suzy calling you Tory. Everyone else calls you Victoria?"

"Well, yes, it's my name, after all."

"Don't get smart," he growled, swotting her bottom.

"I've never liked being called Vicki."

"What about Tory? Do you like that?"

A pang shot through her. "Only Suzy and her parents ever called me that. It made it very special. Now they're all gone."

A brief silence fell.

At last Connor said gruffly, "Tory suits you. Makes me think of the toffee-gold in your eyes. It's much less of a mouthful than Victoria."

"You can call me Tory if you want," she offered.

"I think I will." He looked down at the baby curled against him. "Don't you think so, Dyl?"

Dylan gooed.

Grinning at her, Connor said, "He agrees I should call you Tory."

Still smiling, as Connor disappeared with the baby into the en suite, Victoria thought about the unexpected turn her life had taken.

And the Connor she'd discovered last night had blown her mind. Gentle. Passionate. She'd never intended to sleep with him, but it had been so right. She couldn't bring herself to regret the annihilation of their no-sex pact, even though she suspected last night was going to change everything between them.

For the better.

From the bathroom she could hear the rumble of her lover's deep voice and Dylan's squeals.

He'd assured her he wouldn't leave her high and dry. They had a chance to be the family she'd never dared dream of.

Despite her reservations about herself, about Connor's ability to give her the independence she needed, they really could make this marriage work. At least they both knew exactly where they stood. There were no pretenses. For a brief moment she thought about the fact that she's never told Connor that her eggs had helped Suzy to fall pregnant. That Dylan was part of her. Then she pushed it away. That wasn't really a pretense—she'd kept it secret for Suzy's sake. And she'd never considered herself Dylan's mother—not until Suzy had been killed. But she knew she would have to tell Connor the truth—the sooner the better.

Contentment spread over her as she picked up the paper. The headlines were too depressing; she pulled her face. Her usual favorite, the financial pages didn't draw her as they normally did. She flipped to the middle of the paper, to the personality features. An inset photo drew her eye.

Connor…

In the gossip pages?

The larger surrounding photo was of a laughing couple in wedding dress. She glanced at the caption. "Business as usual?" Dana and Paul had gotten married?

Did Connor know?

She quickly scanned further. The story salaciously rehashed the fact that Dana had been Connor's live-in lover and that her defection to Paul's bed had caused a split in the company.

But it was the concluding paragraph of the story that disturbed Victoria most. The reporter's sly insinuation, that Connor's same-day, low-key wedding had been his way of beating the wedding couple to the church door was given credence by Connor's apparent refusal to comment.

Unmindful of the hiss of the shower and the sounds of glee in the en suite, Victoria set down the paper and stared blindly out of the bedroom window. She didn't even see the first pair of tuis of the spring whistling in the giant pohutukawa in the garden—which would normally have delighted her.

Connor had known that Dana and Paul were getting married yesterday.

Nothing could dislodge that earth-shattering discovery.

Connor had clearly known about the wedding—he'd even been tackily asked to comment. Had last night been about Dana marrying Paul?

A feeling of violation shrouded Victoria. Was it possible that in some twisted way she'd become Connor's instrument of revenge against the couple who'd betrayed him?

No, it wasn't possible. Because *she* had made the choice to move in with him. Not Connor.

But Connor had come up with the idea of marriage....

And deep in her heart she suspected this was the reason why.

He was hurting. Two years on and still he couldn't let it go. Underneath his bitterness at their betrayal must lie an immensely profound love for Dana....

She gave a groan and rolled onto her stomach to bury her face in the soft down pillows.

She needed time to come to terms with this Sunday-morning bombshell. Once she'd recovered from the searing hurt, she'd confront Connor.

But not yet. Not while she felt wounded, raw...and so horribly exposed.

Connor juggled the slippery baby in his arms as water sluiced over them, rinsing off the suds.

Dylan was in heaven, if his squeals and frantic wiggles were anything to go by. Connor had a feeling today's shower was going to become a weekly Sunday-morning ritual.

And damned if he hadn't had fun, too.

He hiked the baby up and gave his sodden head a quick kiss. Soft warmth expanded in his chest.

A part of him.

Dylan was his.

And, God willing, they would have years together. He would watch Dylan grow up and he'd always be looking for parts of himself. Would Dylan's dark-gray baby eyes lighten to the clarity of his? Or would they change to match Suzy's angelic blues?

He was Dylan's daddy. He could hardly wait for Dylan to utter the word. He'd teach it to the baby. But it would take nothing away from Michael.

In asking for his help Michael had given him the greatest gift of all. He'd agreed to be a sperm donor so that the bout of mumps Michael had suffered as a child wouldn't deprive him and Suzy of the child they so desperately wanted.

He would make sure that Dylan grew up knowing everything about Michael. And his mother, too.

Although there were no signs of Suzy in Dylan yet, they would come. With luck the baby had inherited his own height.

"Never fear, you won't be short," he murmured to Dylan who was inquisitively playing with the stream of water that drenched them. "My genes won't allow it."

He grinned. Victoria would claim it was his arrogant gene showing through.

Victoria…

Intertwined with thinking about her sleepy eyes and tousled hair this morning came memories of last night. Her heat, her generosity, her gentle love for his son that contrasted so sharply with her blowtorch sensuality, which had forever altered his perceptions of her.

Dreary?

Not a damn.

Last night he'd gotten a very good feeling about the future. And today he intended to solidify what they already had.

"Ouch," he exclaimed as Dylan grabbed at a sprinkling of chest hair. The baby gave him a grin that was all gums. Connor laughed back, then pinning Dylan securely to his right side, he used his free hand to turn off the faucet.

Dylan protested vocally.

"C'mon, Dylan, time to get Victoria—" He broke off. That

wasn't right. It should be Tory. Come to think of it, he was Dylan's father…his daddy…and he wanted to make that fact public.

Yet according to Dylan's birth certificate his father was listed as Michael.

God, this was getting complicated.…

Dylan's squawks of complaint grew louder.

And as he drew a breath for the next burst, Connor hastily turned the water back on. "Okay, you win, big fella." Connor rather suspected he was creating a problem for next time. "Just a few minutes, right?"

Dylan gurgled with satisfaction.

A bolt of love for the bundle of determination in his arms surged through him. Guardianship and custody were only a part of the complicated ties that bound him to Dylan. Fatherhood was so much more.

A sudden thought startled him. Victoria was more than Dylan's guardian, too. She was also his wife. But not Dylan's mommy.

Yet, although she might not share a biological bond with the baby like he did, Connor knew she loved Dylan.

And he really had no right to the title of Daddy until he'd formalized his relationship with Dylan by adopting him.

It was possible Victoria would want to adopt the baby, too…that way she would become Dylan's mother in fact. Dylan would have a mummy and a daddy.

He bounced Dylan up and down until the baby squealed with laughter. That was something else for them to discuss today. He had great plans for a day on the beach. Building sand castles. A picnic. Paddling in the shallows. And he was determined that he and Victoria would enjoy the day every bit as much as Dylan.

Today. The first day of the rest of their lives. Such a cliché, but so true.

He could barely wait.

* * *

By the time Connor had gotten a now screaming-in-protest Dylan out of the shower and switched off the faucets, Victoria was no longer in the bedroom.

He frowned as he took in the neatly made bed. He'd expected to find her languishing amongst the covers, reading the papers and perhaps sipping a second cup of tea.

But the room was empty.

And only a hint of Victoria's subtle fragrance lingered.

No matter. He'd find her as soon as he'd dressed Dylan, and he'd share what he had planned for the day.

Fifteen minutes later Connor had dressed himself and the baby and come downstairs to find Victoria in the kitchen, buttering a piece of toast. She started as he entered, Dylan riding on his right hip.

He halted in the doorway. "I was going to make breakfast in bed for you."

"I can't stay. Sorry." She gave a rueful shrug. "I need to go to work."

"*Work?*" For the first time he noticed she was wearing black trousers and a crisp white shirt with pin tucks down the front. "Today?"

Her eyes slid away from his. "Bridget called. I need to go into the office."

Disappointment flooded Connor. He'd planned—

The hell with it. It didn't matter a toss what he'd planned. His plans didn't fit with Victoria's goals for her life.

Resentment tasted bitter on his tongue. Last night had given him a false sense of wonder. He'd hoped...

Blast what he'd hoped. Victoria's career would always come first. He'd married her knowing that, so why the hell was he so disappointed?

Because of last night. Because of the way she'd touched

him and responded so sweetly and because of the wonder he'd thought he'd seen in her eyes.

He'd been here before. Yet this time, despite knowing exactly what Victoria's priorities were, despite being armored against her, he'd begun to believe that this time it would be different.

That what they shared was special.

That Victoria was nothing like Dana.

And she was different—he knew she genuinely cared for Dylan, whereas Dana had only ever raised the topic of children as a precursor to a discussion about marriage.

Victoria wasn't manipulative…she wouldn't sleep with him to get a partnership, or beg for a baby when all she wanted was a ring on her finger.

But she did share the same ruthless, single-minded ambition that had driven his ex-lover. And he couldn't help resenting the fact that Victoria would always put work first.

He'd been a victim of—and survived—that vicious circle once. He had no intention of being devastated a second time. And this time it wasn't only his heart at risk. This time there was Dylan—his own son—to consider, too.

He wouldn't—couldn't—allow Victoria to be so cavalier about her responsibility to his baby. *His* baby.

But now was not the time to get into that. Let her go to work. He wasn't about to blurt it all out in a moment of anger. He'd held off telling her that Dylan was his baby this long because she'd been so worried that he intended to take Dylan away from her. He could wait a little longer. Once he'd cooled down he would confront her with his relationship to Dylan—and with what he'd decided to do about it.

It was time for Victoria to learn who called the shots.

"Do what you want," he bit out and swung away.

She shifted from one foot to the other, clearly uneasy. "What are you going to do?"

"What I'd planned." He gave her a look of scorching contempt. "I'm taking Connor to the beach. We'll spend a day doing what families do."

He watched as her eyes darkened and a not-very-nice sense of victory swelled him. She'd made her choice.

And so had he.

Eleven

Over the next week and a half Victoria avoided Connor.

The tightening tension gave her a sense of sitting on the lip of a volcano about to erupt.

Outwardly Connor was civil, and he still read to Dylan every night while she fed the baby his final bottle of the day. But they'd barely spoken since that fateful Sunday morning.

When she met his eyes she could glimpse the gathering turbulence in the darkening storm of gray. There was a confrontation coming and, like the coward she was, she avoided him by using the best excuse she had—work.

As soon as Dylan had eaten breakfast she kissed him goodbye and left him in Anne's capable hands. She came home after a work day and desperately avoided Connor in the evenings—with the exception of Dylan's bedtime. Afterward she retreated to her room—and her laptop.

The crumbling of their truce did little to ease the tension that was building day by day between them.

It all came to a head when Victoria arrived home late one night to find Dylan already asleep—and a glowering Connor waiting for her in the living room, every light blazing.

She came to a halt and set her laptop bag down on one of the leather couches.

Standing there, his legs apart, in a beautifully tailored black business suit and pale-blue shirt sans tie, with his shoes still an impossibly glossy black at the end of a day, he looked formidable. Unreachable. It was impossible to tell whether he felt anything for her at all. Except the anger and annoyance that the harsh overhead lighting revealed so clearly.

"Dylan needs a mother."

Startled by his words, she continued to stare at him.

What did he mean? Anxiety—never far away where Dylan was concerned—pooled in her stomach. Dylan already had a mother.

But she'd never told him….

Had she been too reticent? Was the omission intended to protect Suzy's memory going to cost her dearly?

"Nothing to say?"

The glare he directed at her held anger and frustration and something that was dark and dangerous.

"I had to stay later than—"

"I have a business. I work long hours—but I still have time for Dylan. This is the third time you're late this week—and it's only Wednesday. And last week you were late almost every night, too."

He'd been counting. But instead of making her feel like she was winning this battle of wills between them, a wretched anguish speared her. He didn't think her fit to be a mother.

Her shoulders sagged. Served her right, she supposed. Tonight had been a genuine emergency—the rest of the time she'd been avoiding Connor. She'd been stopping for dinner on the way home so that she didn't have to eat with him and endure the awful estrangement between them, arriving home in time for Dylan's bath and bedtime story. She'd desperately missed out on the extra time with Dylan. But what choice did she have?

Right now she couldn't bear to be anywhere near Connor. It simply hurt too much.

She was trapped between her need to be with Dylan and her desperation to avoid Connor—and protect her breaking heart.

The memory of their night together…of what they might have had…was eating her alive.

Connor was speaking again, the words sharp and cold as hailstones. She pulled herself out of her misery.

"Victoria, if you can't be available for Dylan, if you can't be relied on to be here for the child, then its better you move out."

"*What?*"

Shock caused the blood to drain from her face. She collapsed onto the nearest of the two long, black leather couches, suddenly chilled and weak. "What are you *talking* about?"

"I think you know."

Divorce. He was talking about divorce. "But you promised."

"What?"

"That you wouldn't end it between us." Victoria placed her fingers against her temples, hunching over where she sat as she struggled to gather her thoughts.

She heard his footfalls across the carpet as he moved closer. Those perfectly shiny shoes came into her line of vision. "Things have changed, Victoria."

Dana and Paul had gotten married.

Connor had realized that this fake marriage was never going to be enough for him.

And now he wanted out.

She spoke at his shoes. "You can't do thi—"

"You've hardly been home for Dylan over the past ten days." The words were as harsh as a whip. "You spent last Sunday and most of this past weekend at work."

To avoid him. Because she'd been unable to bear the tension, the antagonism between them. She looked up, her gaze unconsciously pleading with him. "I'll make sure—"

He shook his head. "I'm sorry, Victoria. I have to end this. For Dylan's sake."

His words cut deep into her heart.

If she'd thought the pain unbearable before, she now bled pure grief. This was what she'd feared all along. Marriage to Connor was supposed to have roadblocked this outcome.

The first burst of angry determination fired up. *No.* She wasn't going to let Connor shove her out of Dylan's life because he hadn't gotten the woman he'd really wanted.

She put out of her mind those glorious hours when they'd managed to live together only too well…that magical wedding night that had changed everything between them…that had made it impossible for her to live under the same roof when she knew Connor still loved Dana.

It was unbearable that Dana's wedding had triggered that night of ecstatic passion and incredible emotion. It was worse that he was going to end their arrangement because of a woman who didn't deserve him.

She swallowed the thick ache that misery had lodged in her throat.

"This is all about Dana."

Her voice came out all wrong. Instead of sounding cool and composed, it was an accusatory croak.

"Dana?" He did a wonderful job of looking totally blank.

"Yes, Dana." So he was going to make her spell it out. "Dana, who used to work with you, who used to share your bed—"

"I know who Dana is," he cut in impatiently, putting his hands on his hips and managing to look even more intimidating than ever. "But I fail to see what she has to do with this discussion."

"Everything!" Couldn't he see it? It was so obvious. "She got married last week."

"Yes, I know Dana got married. So what?"

Somehow Victoria didn't think he'd appreciate her telling him he was still hung up on his ex. Especially if he was desperately denying that truth to himself.

Denial was a terrible thing. Ask her, she knew all about that. She'd been telling herself for two years that she disliked Connor, despised him, that he was the most arrogant jerk she'd ever met. When the truth was so much more shameful. She wanted him, she craved him, she'd been wanting to crawl into his bed and do exactly what they had the night of Dana's wedding.

And she'd reveled in every minute of it.

But she wasn't telling him her sordid little secret. "You only married me to get back at Dana."

"That's utter rubbish." His eyes had started to blaze with unfamiliar emotion.

She drew a shaky breath. "It's not rubbish—"

"It's crap." He glared down at her. "We got married because of Dylan. You're making it sound like I'm still hung up on Dana—I'm not."

Maybe she was over-reacting.

According to the newspaper article, he had known Dana and Paul were getting married. No argument there. Victoria tried desperately to regroup her thoughts.

His eyes snapped with fury, and it took all Victoria's determination to carry on with him towering above her like a dark lord full of fury and wrath. But she had to—if she wanted any chance at keeping Dylan.

"But *knowing* that they were getting married is different from living with the *reality* of Dana wedded to Paul." If his love for Dana was anything like the unfurling love she'd discovered for him, that would have been terribly painful. "It took her out of your life permanently. I can understand—"

He edged closer, knee to knee with her now.

"You understand nothing!"

"I can understand," Victoria continued as though he'd never interrupted so rudely, "that you wanted to get back at her. And what better way than by going through with our wedding?"

To Victoria's dismay, he didn't deny it.

After a long moment, she said, "Clearly you've since decided that our marriage isn't what you want." Because Connor loved Dana.

When he finally spoke again his voice was icier than she'd ever heard it. "Spare me the psychobabble. The issue here is not Dana, it's your commitment to Dylan."

Her commitment to Dylan was not in question; he was her child, for heaven's sake. And it was time Connor learned that.

"You don't want to be married to me because I'm not Dana. I can understand that. But you need to understand that I'm not giving Dylan up. He's—"

"I'm not going to give you a choice, Victoria."

"You have to," she said with grim satisfaction. "I'm co-guardian, joint custodian, and I'm—"

"And I am Dylan's biological father!"

Horror struck, she leaped to her feet. They stood face-to-face, both breathing raggedly.

"*You're* Dylan's father?"

He nodded.

"You can't be! *Michael* is his father."

She wanted to howl. It wasn't supposed to be like this. Dylan couldn't be Connor's baby.

Not with everything the way it was between them. The way it had always been, right from that very first meeting when she'd wanted him after one look and he couldn't even remember her darn name. They could not possibly have created together the perfect being that was Dylan.

It was too cruel to be true.

"I'm his biological father. It's my seed that gave him life. And I will do whatever I can to protect him. He's my son."

Just the sound of that possessive claim knocked the bottom out of her world.

Victoria put her fingers to her throbbing temples.

She wasn't giving up her baby. Connor was going to have a fight on his hands like he'd never seen before. The fight for his company against Dana and Paul would be nothing compared to the war she would wage.

She flung her head back, and their gazes locked. "Even if that means throwing out his mother? Yes, I donated the egg that Suzy carried in her body. That makes him part of me. What do you think Dylan will think when he learns about that when he's older?"

Connor's eyes had turned to slits of dark ice. "I don't believe you."

"Why should I lie? It wouldn't get me anywhere." She stood toe-to-toe with him. If she let him win this battle it would be over. She had to convince him. "I can produce the donor agreement to prove that I'm his mother. And you're not kicking me out of my son's life because you've realized you can't get over your worthless lover."

Under her shock and the growing anger there was hurt that he thought her so unworthy of motherhood. But she was dammed if she would let him see how much she cared.

"I'm not in love with Dana," he said into the hush that had fallen.

She studied him, looking for signs of subterfuge. "You don't need to pretend with me."

He grimaced. "I'm not pretending. I got over her a while ago. And it's been surprising to learn how many people think I've had a lucky escape."

A feeling of immense relief fell over her. If he wasn't in

love with Dana, and if they were both Dylan's parents, then there was no reason for him to push her away.

Except that he felt she hadn't been a very good mother....

Victoria sank back onto the couch and dropped her head in her hands. "Dylan is more important to me than anything in the world." Half-fearful of what expression she'd find, she parted her fingers and gazed up at Connor through the gaps.

The cushion lowered as he dropped down beside her. "But what about your job? That's always been your number-one priority." His face was stern, but at least he was listening.

"I love my work, Connor."

How could she explain to him that her work was her security blanket? The thing in life that made her feel worthwhile. He'd think her a total nut.

So instead, she said, "Don't push me out of Dylan's life. He's all I have left of Suzy and he's the only child I'll ever have."

"You should have told me sooner."

"I considered it. But I promised Suzy that I wouldn't tell anyone. I finally convinced myself that you should know. But I couldn't find a way to tell you. What stopped you telling me?"

He shook his head. "At first there was just so much to cope with, I honestly never considered it. Then once you moved in I thought that you were already so stressed that I might take Dylan away from you, that if you knew he was my son you would become even more anxious. I wanted you to settle down a bit before I told you."

"I suppose that's why you're kicking me out now," she said sarcastically.

Connor's expression changed. "Tory—"

Her mobile rang.

"Leave it," he ordered as she dropped onto her knees and rummaged in the side pocket of her laptop bag.

Prickling at the return of his high-handed tone, she said, "I can't. It might be important."

"Work, you mean."

She forced herself to ignore the icily sarcastic jibe and squinted at the face of her cell phone. The number was unfamiliar. And so was the voice that introduced itself as Juliet after she'd said hello.

Listening in absolute silence and in growing guilt to what Juliet had to say, Victoria heard the silent screaming in her head. *Please not this.*

She terminated the call and raised her gaze to Connor's bleak visage.

"My father has had a heart attack."

Connor insisted on accompanying Victoria to the hospital after waking Moni to look after Dylan. It didn't take him long to bundle a rigid Victoria into the Maserati and head for the hospital.

"I haven't seen my father for three years—and I haven't spoken to him in months."

Connor shot a look to Victoria where she sat curled in the passenger seat, her hair tousled and wild against the leather seat back, her eyes dull and staring.

"The conversation ended badly the last time he called."

Her voice was flat and lifeless—nothing like the decisive Victoria he knew. Guilt etched deeply into her pale, drawn features. Empathy for her overwhelmed him. And he wished he could absorb the pain she must be feeling. Coming on top of the crushing shock of Suzy's death, the news of her father's heart attack must be a heavy blow.

He nosed the car into the hospital's underground car park and came around to help her out before putting a hand under her elbow and escorting her into the elevator.

Frank Sutton was still undergoing an emergency angioplasty to open the blocked coronary artery, they were advised by an efficient nurse who sent them to the visitor's waiting room.

As they came through the double doors a woman with a round face and laugh lines leaped to her feet and directed a shaky, uncertain smile at them. "Victoria?"

Victoria moved forward. "Juliet?" At the older woman's nod she said, "Thank you for calling me."

"I tried your home number first, but a disconnect message gave me your cell number." There was a hint of curiosity as Juliet's gaze flickered from Victoria to Connor.

"This is Connor North." Victoria linked her hand through his elbow as she introduced him. Drawing a deep, audible breath, she added in a rush, "My husband."

She hadn't found that easy to admit, Connor realized with grim humor.

"Oh, Frank didn't mention…" Juliet's voice trailed away.

"My father doesn't know yet," Victoria said brusquely. "Do you have any idea when I'll be able to see him?"

"The nurses said it would be a while." After an uncomfortable pause Juliet said, "Frank's been talking about you a lot over the past few weeks."

Tears welled up in Juliet's eyes, and Connor read the discomfort in Victoria's expression. She had no idea of Juliet's role in her father's life, he realized suddenly.

Stepping forward, he said, "There's a coffee dispenser in the corner. What would you each like?"

Both women turned to him with expressions of identical relief. Thank God for coffee. It fixed everything.

"I'll come over and make my own." He should've known that Victoria would be her usual, independent self—even in a time of crisis.

"I'll come, too. Oh, good, there's hot chocolate." Juliet rubbed her hands up and down her arms as though her skin was already too tight. "I don't think I could face caffeine right now."

So he was wrong—and coffee wasn't always the answer.

Especially where human relationships were involved. Connor could only hope that the outcome this time would be happier than it had been for Michael and Suzy. For Victoria's sake, he offered up a desperate prayer for her father to make it safely through without any further complications.

It was three hours before they were allowed to see Frank Sutton. Although the angioplasty had been a success, Victoria was shocked at how much her father had aged since she'd last seen him.

"You came, Victoria!" His eyes lit up as she halted beside his hospital cot.

"Yes, I came," she said lamely. "Juliet called me."

"Ah, Juliet. She's my guardian angel."

"How did you meet her?"

"I started going to church," he replied. "She was one of the first to welcome me." He must've seen her shock because he added, "Hard to believe, I know."

His skin held a yellow cast marred with liver spots that she'd never noticed. He looked old and tired. A broken man. Nothing like the feckless, handsome man who'd ruined her mother's life and made her childhood a battlefield. A sliver of pity pierced her heart.

Whatever he'd done, however enraged and disappointed she'd been with him in the past for failing her, he didn't deserve this.

His hand inched out and closed over hers, the tightening fingers telling her without words of his fear and desperation.

"Frank, this is Victoria's husband, Connor North," Juliet said from the foot of the bed.

Frank lifted his head with a struggle. "You're married?"

And she'd never told him.

It hung between them, yet another recrimination.

Victoria nodded miserably. Connor had been right. She should have invited her father to the wedding, despite their differences.

"Remember my friend Suzy?"

"Of course I remember Suzy. I was sometimes home through the years." His mouth twisted. "Even though you and your mother probably wouldn't believe that, not that I blame either of you," he added as she clenched her fingers under his grip.

"Suzy died in a car accident. Her husband was killed, too." How to explain it? "They had a baby—"

"Oh, poor mite," exclaimed Juliet.

"His name is Dylan…Connor and I were appointed his guardians—"

"And you fell in love." Juliet wore a dreamy expression, and Victoria didn't have the heart to disillusion her.

She searched for something to say that wouldn't make their marriage sound like a cold, convenient arrangement.

Juliet took Frank's other hand. "Your father has been wanting to call you. He's got something to ask you." A smile lit up her cheerful round face, and Victoria found herself warming more and more to the other woman. She had a brisk lightheartedness that was contagious.

"Juliet wants us to get married." Her father's eyes were oddly anxious as he waited for her response.

What did he expect her to do? Refuse permission? She would never do that. Even though she believed Juliet ought to be warned what she was getting herself into.

But it wasn't apprehension that lurked in his eyes. It was something infinitely more basic….

Her father wanted her approval.

Deep within her something gave. He'd never sought her approval before.

"That's wonderful," she said. "When will the wedding be?"

The lines around his eyes eased fractionally. "I've still got to propose. Maybe Juliet won't have me."

"It's been difficult enough to get you to this point, so I'm hardly likely to bolt now." Despite her tart tone, Juliet's eyes overflowed with emotion, tears not far away. "You silly, stubborn man. You had to almost die before you saw sense. Now you'd better hurry up and ask."

"Worried I might croak?"

"Don't joke about dying." Juliet gave a visible shiver then leaned across the bed and brushed her lips across his furrowed brow. "There's nothing remotely funny about it."

"You could do so much better, my dear," Frank whispered and Victoria's own eyes grew dewy.

"Don't sell yourself short, honey." Juliet straightened. "Now hurry up, before the nurse comes back and chases us all out. I've got witnesses now, so you won't be able to back out later."

Victoria exchanged looks with Connor—his eyes were gleaming with humor.

"Juliet, my dear, I've wasted a lot of time because I was afraid I'd let you down. I'm certainly no Romeo, but you will bring light to my life if you marry me."

A funny sensation shot through Victoria.

Juliet loved her father. The emotion in her glowing eyes was unmistakable as she gazed at Frank. But Victoria's stomach hollowed out at the certainty that Juliet was heading for heartbreak.

Her father wasn't capable of living up to anyone's love. He'd even admitted that he hadn't wanted to propose because he knew he would let Juliet down.

Yet before she could protest she heard Juliet reply, "Of course I'll marry you, Frank. Tomorrow if you wish. You only ever had to ask."

Twelve

It was midnight by the time Connor pushed open the front door. The coolness of the night had already settled like a blanket over the house. As they crossed the darkened entrance hall, Victoria finally broke the silence that had clung to her like a heavy pall on the way home.

"You were right," she said listlessly, "I should've invited him—them—to the wedding."

"Victoria, you couldn't have known—"

"He called me. He wanted to see me more often. I told him I didn't believe we could sustain a relationship." She glanced at Connor. "I was afraid, in case he walked away like he'd always done."

"You think he's going to let Juliet down, too, don't you?"

She spread her hands. "I hope not. But I don't know. He doesn't have a good track record at staying—or being responsible. But to be fair, my mother didn't try very hard either.

She just gave up. I thought that was what loving someone meant. Pain and unhappiness."

"Don't underestimate Juliet. There's toughness under that merry cheerfulness."

"She'd better be made of steel to survive my father."

There was no bitterness. It was what she genuinely believed. He considered her. "Frank was a bad father."

"Yes. Between him and my mother, I was determined never to have to rely on someone for money or love. But I don't think they ever loved each other—they got married because of me."

Was that why she was so desperate to be successful? Connor wondered. Or was it independence rather than success that she craved? That rang more true. If she could take care of herself, she wouldn't need to be reliant on a father…or a husband. Suddenly a lot made sense.

It was possible, too, that she saw Dylan as the opportunity to relive her own upbringing. This time with a happy ending.

In a moment of clarity Connor recognized that Victoria had never anticipated a happy ending for herself—her parents had seen to that. Yet she'd married him. He ached for her. She'd chosen to move in with a man she despised rather than leave Dylan vulnerable.

She had backbone all right, this wife of his.

He opened his arms. "Your father is going to be okay. Come, let me hold you."

"I don't know whether my father and I can ever find common ground. But I won't close this door on him again." She came into his arms without hesitation.

Connor started off intending to give comfort, and found instead that by holding her close, her warmth and softness filled a chasm that he hadn't even been aware of having.

Last time she'd asked to be held, he hadn't been ready. He'd been too full of grief.

But now he was ready.

Slowly he inhaled her sweet, feminine scent and realized that he never wanted to let her go. That she had crept into his life, into his heart. That she had become a part of him.

By the time she pulled away, Connor knew that the healing had finally begun.

Victoria stepped into Bridget Edge's office the following morning and shut the door behind her with a gentle thud. She'd given much thought to what she was about to do. After the shock of her father's heart attack and Connor's surprising tenderness in the aftermath, she'd come to the conclusion it was the only option open to her.

Entering the large office that was the domain of the managing partner made her feel a little like a schoolgirl appearing in front of the head mistress. And the steely look in Bridget's gaze did little to ease the butterflies already fluttering in Victoria's stomach.

Taking a deep breath, she said, "Bridget, I've come to give you my resignation."

"Have a seat." Bridget waved to the chair opposite her, barely glancing at the white envelope Victoria set down on the desk. "You're very valuable to us. Why do you want to leave?"

With a sigh, Victoria settled into the chair. "I need some time to straighten my life out. We'll also need to sort out what's to be done about my share in the partnership."

The older woman took off her stylish, dark-rimmed glasses and set them down on her gleaming cherrywood desk. "You've been under a great deal of emotional stress—and your role here at Archer, Cameron & Edge is very demanding."

Victoria nodded, relieved that Bridget understood her position. "I'm failing Dylan, too."

"And Connor North?" Bridget's brows rose. "Where does he fit in?"

That was the most difficult question of all. Victoria wasn't sure of the answer herself.

Oh, Connor. Closing her eyes, she said, "He thinks I'm a terrible mother."

And not the wife he wanted. What was going to happen to their marriage still needed to be resolved, and Victoria wasn't looking forward to that discussion, either. Connor had been tiptoeing around her sensibilities since the news of her father's heart attack, and hadn't raised the subject again. But despite his gentleness, it would have to be dealt with.

Victoria hoped that her resignation from ACE would make Connor reconsider, that it would convince him how seriously she took her commitment to mothering Dylan.

"It's far from easy juggling a demanding career and being the perfect wife and mother. We women have such high expectations of ourselves."

Victoria gave a tired laugh, and opened her eyes. "You can say that again. I had such grand intentions."

"Don't be too hard on yourself, Victoria." Bridget sat forward in her tall leather chair. "It's been a traumatic time for you—inheriting a baby, acquiring a husband and keeping up with your workload. I'm quite a fan of yours, you know."

Staring at Bridget in disbelief, she said slowly, "No, I didn't know. I thought I'd disappointed you, too."

"Not at all." Bridget gave her a smile. "I admired you two years ago when you told me that you were going to be an egg donor so that your best friend could have a baby. You were worried that I would be unhappy because the process would take time from your work."

"Yes." She'd been very concerned. Being a donor had been physically and emotionally taxing and had taken up time that had cut into her workday. "But you never objected once—aside from suggesting that I have counseling to make sure that I would be able to separate myself from the baby once it was born."

"At the time I thought it unlikely that you would ever have children—you didn't seem to have much of a life outside work. I thought that the baby might be your only one."

Victoria watched as Bridget glanced at a photo on her desk, then back at her.

"You probably don't know I was engaged once."

"No, I didn't." Victoria had perceived Bridget as having no life away from ACE Accounting. She couldn't help wondering what had gone wrong with the engagement.

Bridget must have seen the questions in her eyes. "We were touring, on a motorcycle. He drove, I rode pillion. There was an accident—an oncoming driver overtaking recklessly. They told me I was lucky. I broke my back—he died."

The image of Bridget young, on holiday and riding a motorcycle with her lover shifted Victoria's entire perception of her. "I'm so sorry."

"It was almost twenty-five years ago." Bridget gave her a small smile. "I got over it. But, as you may realize, what I have isn't the life I imagined for myself. I pictured myself at fifty-five with a happy marriage, children all grown up and a successful career. I thought I would have it all."

Sadness for the other woman filled Victoria. "Thank you for sharing this."

"I want you to know that I understand a little of what you may be feeling. Loss and emptiness are terrible things. You lost your friend. But you have a baby—and a husband. Enjoy them. Resign if you must. But if your husband knows you as he should, he won't want you to give up your career for him, or even for the baby. If he loves you, he'd want you to find a solution that lets you have it all, without stressing you to death in the process." Another smile softened the words. "But I'll accept your resignation, if that's what you decide *you* really want."

Victoria felt infinitely lighter, as though a load of expectation had been taken from her shoulders. She started to thank Bridget but the other woman interrupted her.

"Of course, there is another option that may bear thinking about. Why don't we rearrange your hours? Perhaps you can come in three days a week? Or five mornings? It'll be easy to organize, now that you've hired a junior accountant to help you."

"But partners have to work full time—it's in my contract," Victoria protested.

"Archer, Cameron & Edge wouldn't want to lose you, Victoria." Bridget gave her a wink. "Particularly when there's a chance that we might secure the account of the Phoenix Corporation. Reducing hours wouldn't even impact on your profit share—I'd make sure of that."

Victoria couldn't help it, she laughed.

"You didn't think this was all about philanthropy, did you?"

But Victoria had seen under the frigid exterior. A bond had been forged between them today that she knew would endure. A peculiar friendship. Bridget was not the hard-nosed harridan she always appeared to be.

Rising to her feet, Victoria picked up the envelope that still lay unopened on the desk. "I'll think about cutting back my hours. It might be a solution." If she could convince Connor that it would give her more time to spend with Dylan, and lessen her office load, there was a possibility that if could work.

Was there a chance that she could truly have it all?

"Good." Bridget picked up her glasses and put them back on. "It will give you a chance to get through this time—and through the next few years." She peered over the rims of her glasses. "I take it you will be having another child or two?"

Victoria gaped. "I—we—haven't talked about that." Connor had been determined to get her out of his life…not pregnant with his baby. That dampened her newly discovered optimism.

Bridget raised her brows. "Well, perhaps it's time you did."

Victoria left work early the next afternoon and dropped by the hospital to be greeted by the news that her father would be discharged the following day.

Both Frank and Juliet were thrilled.

"It's a cause for celebration," said Juliet. "And not the only celebration today, I believe. Surprise!"

Juliet whipped a bunch of wildflowers brightly wrapped in colored cellophane out of the bathroom.

Her father started to sing an off-key "Happy Birthday" and Victoria stared at them both in stunned disbelief.

"How did you…? You remembered," she said, when she found her voice.

"I have a lot to make up for, Victoria. I forgot too many birthdays when you were growing up. Never again." Frank met her eyes squarely. "Sometimes I wasn't even…there."

Victoria didn't want to think back to those days.

Juliet had fallen silent, busying herself in the corner of the room, and Victoria felt a wave of gratitude for the other woman's tact.

"Will you give me a chance to make it up to you?" Frank's expression was uncertain.

He expected her to refuse.

She placed a hand over his. "Of course I will, Dad." It was the first time she'd called him that in years. "A girl can't refuse the chance to be spoilt to death by her father."

"You're worth it, Victoria."

When her father turned away to take a sip of water from the glass on his bedside table, Victoria looked across to Juliet where she stood watching them both, a pleased smile on her face, and mouthed, "Thanks."

She knew exactly who had bought the flowers and made sure that she and her father got the best shot at a reconciliation.

By the time Victoria got home she found Connor dressed in a long-sleeved white shirt that hung out over a pair of well-tailored dark pants. He'd recently shaved and his dark hair was still damp from a shower. He looked utterly divine.

And her heart sank at the realization that he was on his way out.

The only out-of-place note was the baby perched on his arm. Dylan flapped his arms and screeched when he saw her. A tidal wave of love crashed over Victoria.

She crossed the floor in three strides. "It's good to see you, too, sweetie."

He held out his arms and she took him, covering his face with little kisses. "Is that ticklish?" she asked as he giggled and squirmed in her arms. "You and I are going to play this evening."

"Don't make promises you can't keep," said Connor in that deep voice that did illegal things to her heartbeat. "I'm taking you out for dinner."

Victoria lifted her head from the baby's face. "That would be nice."

Nice?

Who was she kidding?

She couldn't wait.

When last had she been out on a date? Usually she used work as an excuse to put men off. She was too busy. She had to be at an audit early the next morning. She had a meeting. She'd used them all.

Work had become her excuse to avoid relationships with men.

Until Suzy and Michael's death had forced her into a building relationship with Connor.

The last time she'd been out to dinner had been with Suzy

and two of her teacher friends, Victoria remembered. A crazy night at an Italian restaurant eating slices of pizza and sipping Chianti and filled with gales of riotous laughter.

For the first time she didn't ache at the memory of Suzy. There was only nostalgia and warmth and a glow of love. The terrible, yawning sense of loss had eased a little. She could think of the good times—there had been so many—without her throat knotting and tears catching her breath.

But she knew going out for dinner with Connor would be nothing like that hilarity-filled evening with Suzy and her friends. Dark excitement curled in her stomach.

"What about Dylan?"

"I've arranged for Anne to come in."

"But doesn't her mother need her in the evenings?"

"I booked a nurse to look after her mother."

"Oh." It was flattering that he'd gone to so much trouble. And that left her with no room for protest. "It looks like you've got everything covered."

"I have." He tossed her a knee-weakening grin. "Give Dylan to me and go shower and get dressed."

Victoria obeyed, feeling like she was stepping into a void.

In the soft glow of the candlelight that gave the restaurant an intimate ambience, Connor studied Victoria. She was wearing a yellow, sleeveless dress with a scooped neck-line that left her shoulders and elegant neck exposed. The golden flame reflected in her eyes, giving them a mysterious sparkle.

He shifted, and keys jingled in his pocket. He wanted to tell her how beautiful she was…how much she meant to him. He didn't know where to start.

"I offered Bridget Edge my resignation today."

Her words shocked him. "You didn't."

She nodded.

"But why?"

For an instant uncertainty glimmered in those lovely eyes. "So that I can spend more time with Dylan. So that you don't divorce me, and take him away."

"Tory!"

"Are you pleased?" She looked worried.

He tried to figure out what he felt. After Michael and Suzy's deaths, he'd hoped that she'd resign and spend all her time with Dylan—like his mother had with him and Brett. Yet now there was only relief at the thought that the terrible pressure that had been on Victoria would ease. What with Suzy and Michael's death, minding a baby, doing a demanding job and now her father's heart attack…something had to give. And he didn't want it to be Victoria who suffered.

But he knew she loved her work—and the independence it gave her—something he hadn't understood when he'd met her two years ago.

"It's not about whether I'm pleased—it's what you want." He chose his words carefully. "If you want to stay home all day with Dylan, you must do so. But if you want to work, then don't feel you need to resign." Had she resigned because she thought that was what he expected? Had he put that much fear into her?

God, he hoped not. That was the last reason in the world he wanted her to do it.

"Bridget was surprised, too."

The waiter chose that moment to bring their meals—Tory's steamed salmon and his steak. Connor waited impatiently for the waiter to finish tending them and leave.

"What did Frigid say?" he asked as he cut his steak.

"Don't call her that," she admonished, "she was very understanding. She suggested that I cut my hours back."

"How do you feel about that?"

Victoria paused to swallow a mouthful of fish. "I think it might be a solution. If I go in the mornings it will give me all afternoon with Dylan."

"Sounds feasible." Already she was looking more at ease. And Connor was delighted.

"I had an interesting day, too." He told her about the visit he'd gotten from the chairman of an infertility support group to whom Suzy and Michael had left a modest legacy. "Turned out that's where they met."

"It was driving me nuts—no one seemed to know."

"They didn't want people to know about what they saw as a humiliating flaw."

"Neither of them were flawed," said Victoria with some heat.

"I couldn't agree more." Connor finished the last bit of steak as Victoria down put her knife and fork. "I thought we might have some dessert."

"That sounds lovely."

But before he could signal to the waiter to bring the dessert menus, he heard someone call his name.

"Connor."

He looked up. Dana was standing next to their table.

"It *is* you. I thought it must be, from the shape of your head." Her gaze went past him and settled on Victoria. "I heard you'd gotten married."

"Dana, our table is ready." Paul came up behind her, and he didn't meet Connor's eyes. "We need to go through."

She pouted prettily. "Soon, darling." And turned back to Connor. "I didn't think you'd ever marry."

"The right woman came along."

Annoyance flared in the dark-blue eyes. "How romantic, darling. I want to hear everything." She shifted into the booth beside him, her black dress hiking up, and a stockinged thigh brushed his.

Instead of desire, all he felt was distaste.

By contrast, Victoria was smiling up at Paul and shaking hands as they introduced themselves. Elegant, gracious Victoria.

His wife.

Connor moved away from Dana imperceptibly.

Her hand landed on his thigh, high enough for her intent to be obvious. His distaste grew more pronounced.

"We came out to celebrate tonight," said Paul. "Dana's pregnant—she had a scan today."

"A baby? How lovely." But Victoria was looking at him, her hazel eyes velvety with concern.

"I always wanted a baby. Didn't I, Connor darling?"

A wedding ring, more like. Threaded through his nose. Marriage to a wealthy man and a generous prenuptial contract had figured heavily in Dana's goals. Her own success had not been enough. She had craved more. More money. More status. More power.

He met Paul's gaze. "I wish you both every happiness."

The tension in Victoria's shoulders eased a little.

She'd obviously been worried he might create a scene. He wanted to reassure her, tell her that Dana truly meant nothing to him.

He smiled at her instead, a slow, sensual smile, and watched as awareness flared in her eyes. Heat spread through him. He suppressed a silent groan. What had he started?

"Does Victoria know you don't intend to have children?" Dana's comment was as unwelcome as a bucket of cold water.

But Victoria only arched a well-shaped brow. "I don't think it's true that Connor never wanted children. Otherwise, why did he choose to become a sperm donor?"

Connor tried very hard not to laugh. It made him sound like he'd done it for a living. Victoria was outrageous.

Dana's mouth had fallen open. Even Paul looked startled.

"Connor donated sperm?"

"You didn't know?" Victoria did great work of looking amazed. "Connor and I donated so that friends of ours could have the child of their dreams, didn't we, Connor darling?" She drawled *darling* in a wicked imitation of Dana's use of the endearment, and Connor bit down on the fierce urge to laugh.

"That was very generous—of both of you."

"Suzy was my best friend. That's what you do for friends, help make their dreams come true." She gave an angelic smile as she encountered Connor's arrested gaze. He wondered if only he knew that she was actually chastising Paul.

"Do you often see the child?" Paul looked sheepish.

"His parents were killed and—"

"—we decided to adopt him, didn't we, Victoria?" He knew it was wrong to railroad her into something they hadn't even discussed. But the last thing in the world he wanted was a divorce. He'd be foolish to let Victoria slip away.

"Er…yes." Her eyes lit up with joy.

"So you only got married because of the child?" Dana had been silent, obviously thinking it through. Now her features relaxed in relief.

"Isn't that why many couples get married?" Connor gave the other couple a narrow stare. Paul glanced away first. "But at least I wasn't trapped into a marriage I didn't want." In spite of the fury that glittered in Dana's eyes, Connor didn't feel the satisfaction he'd expected as he made the comment. He had no need to pay either of them back further for what they'd done to him—they'd landed in a hell of their own making. With its huge mortgage that house would be a noose around their necks, and no doubt Paul was still struggling to service the interest on the loan he'd taken to pay Connor out for his share of Harper-North.

"Marrying Victoria is the best decision I've ever made," he continued softly, reaching over to stroke Victoria's hand.

Dana rose to her feet with an angry rustle of taffeta. "We should be on our way."

Paul's expression was far from happy. "Nice meeting you,"

he said to Victoria, and she smiled back at him as Paul sidled out of the booth.

Connor couldn't help thinking that even Paul knew who had gotten the better deal. And it wasn't Paul.

Thirteen

When they arrived home it was late, and Dylan was asleep. After seeing Anne out, Connor locked the front door and Victoria headed for the stairs.

"Victoria…"

She froze on the first step as Connor's deep voice cut into the night. He came up behind her, his breath warm on her bare shoulders. "I forgot to give you your birthday gift."

Swinging around, she saw with a shock that he was very close. Standing on the step put her directly at eye level with him. She took the flat parcel that he offered.

"Thank you—you didn't need to do it." She gave him a bright smile. "But it's very much appreciated." Turning, she ran lightly up the stairs, through the sitting room that adjoined her room with the nursery, into her bedroom.

"Aren't you going to open it?"

She hadn't heard him come up behind her. Drawing a deep

breath, she hoped that he wouldn't hear the thunder in her heart as she turned around.

"Yes, yes, of course."

Her fingers were trembling as she untied the ribbons. The gay wrapping paper fell away to reveal a picture frame. She turned it over and found herself looking into four smiling faces under the arch of a church door.

"You remember that photo, don't you?" Connor was much too close. "You even told me to smile."

"I remember." A soft ache welled up as Victoria stared into Suzy's beloved face…and then moved on to Michael's grin. Flanking Michael, even Connor's hard face wore a smile.

"We all look so happy."

"That's how Suzy and Michael would want us to remember them," he said.

She swung around to face him. "Thank you for this. You couldn't have given me a better present." She flung her arms around his neck, the frame dangling over his shoulder, and kissed him.

After a moment he kissed her back.

"Tory!"

She pulled away and looked into the face that had become as familiar as her own. The hewn cheekbones, the bladed nose and those penetrating eyes.

Connor wasn't her father.

There wasn't a neglectful, irresponsible bone in his body. He'd done everything he could to give Dylan a future that would be secure. And he'd always been there for her.

She owed him an apology. "I'm sorry for believing that you were a jerk."

"Oh, Tory." His hands tightened on her bare arms. "And I'm sorry for believing you were dull and dreary."

"*What?*"

His eyes laughed down into hers.

"I know. I don't know how I came up with that." This time the kiss was deep and very, very hot. By the time it was over they were both breathless.

He took the photo frame from her and set it down carefully on the dressing table.

Then he returned to her.

"We're going to make love," he told her. "No casual encounter. And this time you're going to stay—no rushing off before I let you go."

"Never again," she vowed.

"Oh, God, Tory."

She curved into him, her body so close that she could feel the outline of his chest muscles against her. "I'm staying right here."

"Forever."

"If you want."

"I want."

His fingers pulled down the zipper at the back of her dress. She shimmied out of it and it fell in a pool on the carpet.

He'd trodden out his shoes and unbuttoned the top two buttons of his shirt, and now he pulled the white shirt over his head. He stepped out of his pants a moment later. He wore only close-fitting boxers, and the sight of his hard, muscled body gave her a secret thrill.

Victoria kicked off her heels.

And trembled a little with anticipation as his arms came around her and he undid the hooks of the white lacy bra that she wore. He skimmed his hands over her hips, sweeping the brief bits of lace down her legs, leaving her naked to his ravenous gaze.

A moment later he was naked, too.

The hard ridge of his erection revealed how much he desired her. And he swept her into his arms and lowered her onto the queen bed.

"This is going to be over way too fast," he murmured into her ear. "I want you so badly."

He licked the shell-like shape of her ear and Victoria shivered with delight.

But despite his forecast he stretched the pleasure forever. He used his hands, and his lips, and his tongue to bring Victoria to heights that she'd never experienced.

When he finally parted her legs, she was on fire for him.

Connor positioned himself over her and drove deep.

She closed her eyes and let the passion take her. Her fingertips dug into his shoulders. He gasped and drove again.

Arching beneath him, Victoria found the rhythm. And then they were moving in unison, as one.

The pleasure rose in a bright, blinding arc. And as the light exploded behind her eyes, she heard Connor whisper, "I love you, Tory. How I love you."

The words tilted her into a dizzying whirl of color and ecstasy that seemed to go on forever. And she found herself gasping, "I love you, too."

Afterward they lay on their backs on the bed, their hunger for each other temporarily sated.

"Did you mean what you said?" she asked, turning her head to meet his warm eyes.

"That I love you?"

She nodded.

"Of course I did."

She gave him a slow, dreamy smile. "I love you, too. I've been thinking, Connor. That billion-dollar baby bargain of yours? I got the best bargain of all—as well as Dylan, I got you."

"Nah." He shook his head. "I definitely did better out of it. I got you, when I might have ended up with Dana in the greatest mistake of my life. My guardian angel must've been looking out for me."

"You believe in angels?"

He nodded solemnly. "Falling in love did that for me."

"I like the idea of Suzy as an angel." Victoria glanced at the photo on her dressing table. "I can see her wearing a halo on her curls, smiling that sweet smile of hers."

"With Michael beside her, holding her hand."

"Of course."

"They'd be happy for us, you know."

Victoria nodded. "I think so, too."

"They tried to match-make us two years ago—I was furious about it."

"I'm not surprised! You'd just been through a bad experience with Dana. It wasn't the right time."

"And you didn't like me," he said righteously. "You thought I was a jerk that no sane woman could live with. Yet look at you now."

"I didn't know you!" she corrected, laughing at him.

He bent forward and placed a kiss on the tip of her nose. "So you think you know me now?"

Victoria nodded. "To know you is to love you."

"Oh, Tory." He pulled her into his arms and kissed her. "I'll never tire of hearing that, of kissing you, of making love to you."

"I suppose that means that there will have to be a little brother or sister for Dylan one day." Her eyes turned a wicked gold.

"That sounds like a great idea." Connor laughed silently, happiness and joy filling him. "But we'll need to practice."

"So what are we waiting for?" his wife asked, pulling his head down to hers.

Epilogue

Frank and Juliet's wedding took place at Victoria and Connor's home.

And Victoria disgraced herself by crying buckets. But she didn't care. Nor did the man who stood proudly beside her, holding her hand.

They were both happy.

And so were the bridal couple.

"Just know that it's not that I don't adore you. I do," she sobbingly assured a radiant Juliet.

"It's true," Connor assured her.

Juliet laughed and patted her on the shoulder.

On the pretext of fetching a tissue, Victoria rushed upstairs and washed her face with cool water. She returned to the large deck onto which the reception rooms had been flung open, where a trio of musicians played festive songs. The evening was clear, and the first stars were starting to show. Lights flickered romantically in the trees while candles floated on the swimming pool.

Victoria couldn't suppress a smile at the sight of Anne restraining Dylan as he leaned toward the flames on the water's surface, gurgling with pleasure.

"Okay?" Connor asked her, coming up behind her and placing an arm around her shoulder.

She gave one last sniff. "I'm fine. I always cry at weddings."

"I remember. You cried at Suzy and Michael's wedding. But you didn't cry at ours." He placed a finger under her chin and gave her a searching glance. "Any reason for that?"

"Because I was terrified that once I started I wouldn't be able to stop."

He opened his arms and she stepped into them. "I'm still here."

"Don't," she whispered, "you'll set me off all over again."

He shuffled his feet and she followed his lead. It looked to all the world as if they were dancing.

"I love your happy tears. Don't store them up, you should release them."

"I'd drown you." She gave him a weak smile.

He smiled back. "Do your worst, I don't scare easily."

Oh, Connor.

This was when he turned her heart to mush. Wordlessly, she snuggled up to him and let the music take her to a quiet place where only she and Connor, with his arms around her and his body close to hers, existed.

When the song came to an end they made their way to the pool. Dylan saw them approaching and shrieked happily.

This was her family, her home. As the next melody started to play, Victoria knew that her life was complete, she had it all.

* * * * *

Don't miss Tessa Radley's
next Silhouette Desire release,
on sale December 8, 2009.

Celebrate Harlequin's 60th anniversary with
Harlequin® Superromance® and the
DIAMOND LEGACY miniseries!

Follow the stories of four cousins as they come
to terms with the complications of love
and what it means to be a family.
Discover with them the sixty-year-old secret
that rocks not one but two families in...
A DAUGHTER'S TRUST
by Tara Taylor Quinn.

Available in September 2009 from
Harlequin® Superromance®

RICK'S APPOINTMENT with his attorney early Wednesday morning went only moderately better than his meeting with social services the day before. The prognosis wasn't great—but at least his attorney was going to file a motion for DNA testing. Just so Rick could petition to see the child…his sister's baby. The sister he didn't know he had until it was too late.

The rest of what his attorney said had been downhill from there.

Cell phone in hand before he'd even reached his Nitro, Rick punched in the speed dial number he'd programmed the day before.

Maybe foster parent Sue Bookman hadn't received his message. Or had lost his number. Maybe she didn't want to talk to him. At this point he didn't much care what she wanted.

"Hello?" She answered before the first ring was complete. And sounded breathless.

Young and breathless.

"Ms. Bookman?"

"Yes. This is Rick Kraynick, right?"

"Yes, ma'am."

"I recognized your number on caller ID," she said, her voice uneven, as though she was still engaged in whatever physical activity had her so breathless to begin with. "I'm sorry I didn't get back to you. I've been a little…distracted."

The words came in more disjointed spurts. Was she jogging?

"No problem," he said, when, in fact, he'd spent the better part of the night before watching his phone. And fretting. "Did I get you at a bad time?"

"No worse than usual," she said, adding, "Better than some. So, how can I help?"

God, if only this could be so easy. He'd ask. She'd help. And life could go well. At least for one little person in his family.

It would be a first.

"Mr. Kraynick?"

"Yes. Sorry. I was…are you sure there isn't a better time to call?"

"I'm bouncing a baby, Mr. Kraynick. It's what I do."

"Is it Carrie?" he asked quickly, his pulse racing.

"How do you know Carrie?" She sounded defensive, which wouldn't do him any good.

"I'm her uncle," he explained, "her mother's—Christy's— older brother, and I know you have her."

"I can neither confirm nor deny your allegations, Mr. Kraynick. Please call social services." She rattled off the number.

"Wait!" he said, unable to hide his urgency. "Please," he said more calmly. "Just hear me out."

"How did you find me?"

"A friend of Christy's."

"I'm sorry I can't help you, Mr. Kraynick," she said softly. "This conversation is over."

"I grew up in foster care," he said, as though that gave him some special privilege. Some insider's edge.

"Then you know you shouldn't be calling me at all."

"Yes… But Carrie is my niece," he said. "I need to see her. To know that she's okay."

"You'll have to go through social services to arrange that."

"I'm sure you know it's not as easy as it sounds. I'm a single man with no real ties and I've no intention of petitioning for custody. They aren't real eager to give me the time of day. I never even knew Carrie's mother. For all intents and purposes, our mother didn't raise either one of us. All I have going for me is half a set of genes. My lawyer's on it, but it could be weeks—months—before this is sorted out. Carrie could be adopted by then. Which would be fine, great for her, but then I'd have lost my chance. I don't want to take her. I won't hurt her. I just have to see her."

"I'm sorry, Mr. Kraynick, but…"

* * * * *

*Find out if Rick Kraynick will ever have
a chance to meet his niece.
Look for A DAUGHTER'S TRUST
by Tara Taylor Quinn,
available in September 2009.*

We'll be spotlighting a different series
every month throughout 2009
to celebrate our 60th anniversary.

Look for Harlequin® Superromance®
in September!

*Celebrate with
The Diamond Legacy
miniseries!*

Follow the stories of four cousins as they come to terms
with the complications of love and what it means to
be a family. Discover with them the sixty-year-old secret
that rocks not one but two families.

A DAUGHTER'S TRUST by *Tara Taylor Quinn*
September

FOR THE LOVE OF FAMILY by *Kathleen O'Brien*
October

LIKE FATHER, LIKE SON by *Karina Bliss*
November

A MOTHER'S SECRET by *Janice Kay Johnson*
December

Available wherever books are sold.

From *New York Times* bestselling authors

CARLA NEGGERS
SUSAN MALLERY
KAREN HARPER

More Than Words:
STORIES OF STRENGTH

They're your neighbors, your aunts, your sisters and your best friends. They're women across North America committed to changing and enriching lives, one good deed at a time. Three of these exceptional women have been selected as recipients of Harlequin's More Than Words award. And three *New York Times* bestselling authors have kindly offered their creativity to write original short stories inspired by these real-life heroines.

Visit **www.HarlequinMoreThanWords.com** to find out more, or to nominate a real-life heroine in your life.

Proceeds from the sale of this book will be reinvested in Harlequin's charitable initiatives.

Available in March 2009 wherever books are sold.

Stay up-to-date on all your romance reading news!

The Harlequin Inside Romance newsletter is a **FREE** quarterly newsletter highlighting our upcoming series releases and promotions!

Go to
eHarlequin.com/InsideRomance
or e-mail us at
InsideRomance@Harlequin.com
to sign up to receive
your **FREE** newsletter today!

You can also subscribe by writing to us at: HARLEQUIN BOOKS
Attention: Customer Service Department
P.O. Box 9057, Buffalo, NY 14269-9057

Please allow 4-6 weeks for delivery of the first issue by mail.

IRNBPAQ209

COMING NEXT MONTH
Available September 8, 2009

#1963 MORE THAN A MILLIONAIRE—Emilie Rose
Man of the Month
The wrong woman is carrying his baby! A medical mix-up wreaks havoc on his plans, and now he'll do anything to gain custody of his heir—even if it means seducing the mother-to-be.

#1964 TEXAN'S WEDDING-NIGHT WAGER—
Charlene Sands
Texas Cattleman's Club: Maverick County Millionaires
This Texan won't sign the papers. Before he agrees to a divorce, he wants revenge on his estranged wife. But his plan backfires when she turns the tables on him....

#1965 CONQUERING KING'S HEART—Maureen Child
Kings of California
Passion reignites when long-ago lovers find themselves in each other's arms—and at each other's throats. Don't miss this latest irresistible King hero!

#1966 ONE NIGHT, TWO BABIES—Kathie DeNosky
The Illegitimate Heirs
A steamy one-week affair leaves this heiress alone and pregnant—with twins! When the billionaire father returns,
will a marriage by contract be enough to claim his family?

#1967 IN THE TYCOON'S DEBT—Emily McKay
The once-scorned CEO will give his former bride what she wants...as soon as she gives him the wedding night he's long been denied.

#1968 THE BILLIONAIRE'S FAKE ENGAGEMENT—
Robyn Grady
When news breaks of an ex-lover carrying his child, this billionaire proposes to his mysterious mistress to create a distraction. Yet will he still want her to wear his ring when she reveals the secrets of her past?